THE
WAR
BELOW

Also by Marsha Forchuk Skrypuch

Making Bombs for Hitler

THE
WAR
BELOW

A novel by

MARSHA FORCHUK SKRYPUCH

SCHOLASTIC PRESS | NEW YORK

Library of Congress Cataloging-in-Publication Data available

ISBN 978-1-338-23302-5

10 9 8 7 6 5 4 3 2 1   18 19 20 21 22

Printed in the U. S. A.   23

First American edition, May 2018

Book design by Yaffa Jaskoll

TO PETER J. POTICHNYJ,
MY INSPIRATION FOR LUKA
—M.S.

CHAPTER ONE
CHILL

The corpses around me provided an odd sort of comfort. These people had been my friends and fellow captives. We had worked alongside each other during long, harsh months in the Nazi slave camp, helping each other when we could.

Above me was Josip, who had been injured with me in the bomb blast at the factory. In life, he'd tried to protect us younger boys from the harshest jobs, and now, in death, his body was my shield.

Below me were two women and one man who had all died slowly from lack of food. I felt guilty, lying on top of them. They deserved more respect than that, but would I have been smothered if I had hidden any deeper in this death wagon? I said a silent prayer for their souls.

Shuffling footsteps close by . . .

I held my breath and closed my eyes. I forced my face to take on the slackness of death. The canvas rustled as it was pulled aside and I tried not to flinch as a beam of light penetrated my eyelids. A guttural grunt. Canvas rustling back in place, returning the truck bed to a welcome darkness.

The *snick* of a truck door opening and the *smack* of it closing. The engine roaring to life and the smell of diesel fuel. We were moving. But within moments the truck idled to a stop, the engine still grumbling. Fear threatened to grip me, but I had no time for that. What if the canvas was opened again? I had to look dead. Forcing my body into limpness, I closed my eyes once more.

An exchange of laughter and words in German between the driver and someone else—likely one of the guards at the gate. I held my breath and emptied my mind, then waited for what seemed like an eternity, but was probably only a minute.

The truck engine roared once again, and we were moving. Relief washed over me, but I knew that my challenges had just begun.

I had to get out of this truck once it was a kilometer or two away from the camp. If I was still here when it got to its destination, I would be burned alive.

I gently rolled Josip's body away from me and tried to sit up, but I was stiff and chilled and dizzy. I wore nothing but a thin hospital gown, and the jagged row of stitches holding together the wound in my thigh throbbed. The truck pitched and bumped along the bomb-pitted road and I felt queasy from the sweet smell of the corpses.

Crawling amidst the dead, I got to the back of the truck bed and shifted onto my knees. The canvas was tied from the outside, so I worked one arm through where the fabric ended and groped around for the knotted rope outside. As the driver swerved and swayed, probably trying to miss the bigger holes in the road, I grabbed on to the side of the truck bed so I wouldn't fall, and worked at loosening a single knot. It had begun to rain, making it hard to get a grip on the rope, but finally I managed to loosen the canvas enough.

I squeezed my body out between the canvas and the metal, balanced my bare feet on a tiny bit of ledge, and took in one long gulp of cold, clean air. Rain washed over me.

My plan was to hold on and prepare for a careful fall, but just then the truck hit a pothole. I flew through the air and crashed down in the darkness.

CHAPTER TWO
STARS

A plop of rain landed on my nose. My eyes flew open but my arms and legs refused to move. Where was I? The star-peppered sky loomed huge above me. One of the stars grew bigger and brighter and that's when I truly woke up.

It was heading right for me.

My muscles screamed as I rolled off the road and fell down into a ditch. The ground shook as the bomb hit, frighteningly close. Ignoring the pain, I pulled myself onto my feet. Where I had lain just seconds ago was now a smoking pit.

A bigger bomb landed somewhere in the distance, lighting up the farmers' fields and a patchwork of familiar factories up ahead.

Another white explosion on the road. My knees buckled and I fell to the ground.

What madness had made me escape the labor camp?

Yes, life had been harsh there and yes, people like me who were given the worst jobs rarely survived. But my friend Lida was back there. Maybe I should have stayed in the hospital. Maybe they wouldn't have killed me.

Poor Lida. Even though she had urged me to go, I felt like such a bad friend for deserting her.

She thought of me as her big brother Luka and I loved her with all my heart. Was she sleeping safe in her barracks right now? I hoped that she would understand why I had no choice. Josip hadn't been badly injured, yet the care he received hadn't made him any better. I didn't trust them at the hospital. So when the chance came for me to get out, I had to do it. Maybe Lida would escape somehow as well.

Surely the war would end soon, and I had to get back to Kyiv to find my father. I'd walk the whole way there if I had to.

Lida would have to understand. "Stay safe, dear Lida," I prayed. "We will meet again, either here or in the next world . . ."

As another bomb exploded somewhere in the distance and the sky lit up again, I saw a range of mountains far away. Nearer to me, there were brown fields, slick with rain. I had my bearings. I was about two kilometers away from the work camp.

Before I had been injured, I'd ridden a crowded train each day into the city and those train tracks were parallel to the road the truck had taken. It was where I and other slave laborers had worked twelve-hour shifts in a metalworks factory, making bomb parts. Most mornings we were too tired and hungry to say much to each other, but once, Josip had pointed out the train window. "Those mountains, Luka," he'd said. "They connect to our own Carpathians."

Another worker had grunted in agreement. "Too bad they're so far away."

The bombs stopped and blackness descended once again. I ran the palm of my hand down the ragged wound on my leg. Some of the stitches had opened up, but the wound itself did not seem to be bleeding. I could feel the sting of scrapes along my spine and shoulders, but as I flexed and stretched, I realized how lucky my fall had been. Mud is softer than dry road, after all. I forced myself to stand, and headed for the field.

My bare feet sank into the stony muck of a farmer's field and it took much effort to pull them out and keep on walking. I found a sturdy branch and used it as a staff. It sank deep into the mud too, but it was better than nothing. The wound throbbed and I was chilled from the rain, but

I focused on putting one foot in front of the other. I had to hide before daylight.

Just then I heard the rumbling of a truck coming down the road. I threw myself down into the muck. I didn't have to see it to know that the truck was filled with Nazi soldiers on patrol.

When the truck was past me, I got back up and slowly, carefully, with the mountains as my beacon, trudged on. I knew I couldn't get to the mountains right away, but by keeping them in sight, at least I'd be walking away from the slave-labor camp and away from the city. That was all I could think of.

As my eyes got used to the darkness and my head cleared from the fall, I realized that I wasn't stepping only on mud and stones, I was walking through a giant vegetable field! I fell to my knees, scraped through the mud, and found what I thought was a weighty potato bigger than my fist.

Memories filled my imagination—fresh *pyrohy* drizzled with bacon fat, a dollop of sour cream on the side. Mama's smiling face . . .

I took a big bite. Bitter and all too familiar. Not a potato at all, but a turnip. Of all the fields in the Reich, why did I end up in one filled with turnips? At the camp, we'd had watery turnip soup each and every day. At least this was a fresh turnip, almost sweet, not old and cooked to mush. And it was, after all, food.

The sky lit up for a single second. Those mountains were so far away, but they were my link to home. Were the Nazis there as well? It was rough terrain, hard to navigate if you weren't a local. Maybe they had left the mountains free.

I couldn't finish the entire turnip but didn't want to throw it away, so I carried what was left and kept trudging on, hoping to find a good hiding place.

A sudden stab of pain in my heel. My knees buckled and I fell down into the muck. I ran my fingertips over my heel and pulled out a shard of glass, throwing it angrily into the field.

Ignoring the pain, I squeezed the injured flesh as if it were a pimple, to make the blood gush out. It hurt, but I kept on squeezing because I could feel a bit of glass still lodged in there and I wouldn't be able to put my heel down as long as it was there. Finally, I felt a sliver ooze out. I flicked it away, then pushed around on the wound, searching for more, but I had gotten it all. I propped my injured foot up with my other knee and let the blood drip down as I racked my brain, wondering what I should do next.

You have the tools to heal yourself. My father's voice, from the depths of my memory.

I closed my eyes and thought of him. Tato wasn't the kind of person who gave up.

"Do they expect me to destroy all my medicines and my books?" he says to Mama. *"These took me years to collect and formulate. I can help many people—especially now that we're at war."*

"You'll be arrested for hoarding," says Mama. *"You know what the Soviet police said—we must destroy everything before the Nazis invade Kyiv."*

"So we Kyivans are not worth saving?"

"Please, Volodya, just do as they say."

"If I do, people will die."

The next day, Tato grips my hand and Mama's as we stand in the street, watching Sasha and Misha, two local bullies who now wear NKVD uniforms, smash in our windows and toss out Tato's precious collection of natural-remedy books. They rip his handwritten journal and toss it onto the pile of books in the street and then set it on fire. As the books burn, they throw his tinctures into the fire. How I hate these Communist Secret Police.

"I don't need those things," Tato says too loudly. *"I can heal people without them."*

And he does. Using items at hand—boot black and cobwebs and birch leaves and nettle—he teaches me his techniques. He keeps on helping people until one of our neighbors accuses him of being a Nazi spy.

Sasha, dressed in his uniform, comes to our door. We have no idea what he is looking for. Haven't they already destroyed everything of value?

But as they move shelves and look in hiding spots, a chill goes through me. Tato has hidden a leather-bound remedy book that has been passed down from healers in our family, one generation to the next, for hundreds of years. I am amazed at the detailed drawings of herbs and flowers and the funny script that looks like it has been written with a paintbrush. The book was written by a German nun in the Middle Ages. It has nothing to do with the Nazis.

"I knew it!" shouts Sasha, yanking the fragile old book out of a deep drawer. "This is in German."

He tears it to shreds, scattering bits of paper all over our floor and onto the front step. He puts handcuffs on Tato's wrists and parades him through the streets as a traitor.

And then Tato disappears . . .

I opened my eyes and tried to think like Tato.

The mud.

I plunged my hand deep into the muck and pulled out a fairly solid and drier chunk of soil. I crumbled it, then applied it to my heel, soaking up the excess blood. After a minute, I scraped the mud off and replaced it with a fresh handful, making sure to pack it right into the cut to stanch the bleeding. I tore off a strip of cloth from my gown and bound my heel as tightly as I could.

I got up and continued walking, limping and leaning heavily on the stick, barely noticing the cold and rain.

As dawn broke, I noticed an odd sparkling up ahead. Fragments of glass clinging to the skeleton of a long, low building. Huge jagged shards sticking up in the muddy ground. That one shard of glass that I'd stepped on had traveled a long way from the explosion, and I realized how lucky I had been. What if I had stepped on all these shards in the dark? My feet would have been sliced open and I would have bled to death on the spot.

I kept my distance from the building and continued walking. All at once I realized: This had been a greenhouse. There might still be some berries or vegetables mixed with the glass. My mouth watered at the thought. But it didn't matter now—it was all destroyed. I didn't blame the British and Americans for bombing German farms. Maybe if their soldiers couldn't eat, they'd stop fighting. I just wished there were a way to bomb the Nazis without bombing their prisoners.

I kept on going—on the lookout for a barn or haystack—anyplace where I could collapse and hide.

Just when I was nearly beyond exhaustion, the field

gave way to a rolling grassy area. I hobbled to the top of a small knoll. Before me stood a large farmhouse that had seen better days. Its windows were covered with tar paper—that was a good thing, seeing as I would have been in full view from where I stood.

Near the farmhouse were a couple of buildings. The one closest to it had a bombed-in roof. Between me and the buildings was a trough with a water pump. I was tempted to pump myself some water—I would have loved a drink. But I couldn't risk it.

I ducked behind the closest building. The sky lit up for a moment from a distant explosion, revealing a barn on the other side of the grassy area. It was weather-worn but sturdy. No bomb had damaged it yet.

I limped across the yard to the barn's small side door. I lifted the latch and waited, holding the door open just a crack. If there was a dog in there, I wanted to know about it before I went in.

One second . . . Two . . . Three.

No dog.

I stepped inside.

CHAPTER THREE
WARMTH

The warm air was a relief, but my nose nearly closed up with the ripe smell of animal dung. As my eyes adjusted to the dimness, I saw a pair of eyes staring out at me from one of the stalls. The others seemed to be empty. The eyes were not frightened but inquisitive. I hobbled over and reached out my hand so the horse would know I didn't mean it any harm. It sniffed my palm, then rubbed its face against my neck. It inhaled, shuddered, sneezed—getting horse snot all over me. It was so unexpected that I nearly laughed out loud. I leaned into the horse's warmth and closed my eyes, feeling almost safe.

Memories flooded in of when I was young, of my grandfather's farm beyond the woods outside of Kyiv. On Sundays, before Tato was arrested, we would go for a visit once we'd tended to our own small garden.

Old farmers like him who weren't working communally on the *kolkhoz* lived simply. But he did have a swayback mare named Kulia—or "Bullet"—even though she was anything but speedy. Once, Tato had lifted me onto the old mare's back. It was so high up that I was terrified at first, but Kulia just stood there, tolerating me. Her gray mane stuck up in all directions like Baba Yaga's hair in the old tales. I tried to comb it down with my fingers, but they just got stuck in the knots. So I leaned forward and hugged Kulia's neck, feeling safe.

"Is your name Kulia?" I whispered to the German horse now. She leaned in and licked some of the mud off my cheek. I offered her the rest of my turnip. She sniffed it, wrinkled her nose, then licked my cheek again. This horse had good taste. She knew that even mud was preferable to too much turnip.

I heard a low breathing from the shadows, so I ventured down the length of the barn until I came face-to-face with a mangy white cow.

"Hi, Beela," I said, scratching the bony ridge between her ears. "We're going to be friends, aren't we?" I held my other hand up to her nose. She sniffed, then looked up at me with trusting eyes. I took that as a yes.

Once I was fairly certain that the animals were

comfortable with my presence, I looked around the barn and heard my father's voice in my mind, just as if he were right beside me: *You have the tools to heal yourself.*

There was a bundle of hay in front of each animal, but no water. In the shadows across from Kulia's stall, I found a bin of oats with a wooden scoop. I grabbed one handful and poured them into my mouth, but when I tried to chew, I nearly broke a tooth, so I spat them out.

I tried to look at this barn with my father's eyes. What did it contain that I could use?

A cow. Cows give milk.

Footsteps sounded at the front of the barn. I stood still. The person outside whistled a tuneless melody.

Where could I hide? Wooden stairs led up—probably to the hayloft. Not the best hiding place, but it would have to do. I climbed the stairs, dragging my injured foot. I settled into a dark corner behind one of the bales and hugged my knees to my chest.

Before our pharmacy was destroyed, Tato had begun to teach me his craft. Not only how to compound medications with store-bought items, but also how to use the gifts of nature. To keep a wound clean, salt water worked wonders, and so did honey, but if you had nothing else, you had to improvise. A piece of moldy bread was the best, or a cloth soaked in whey. Fresh cow's milk was also good. But would I be able to get some from the cow down below without being caught?

The barn doors scraped open and the entry to the loft became visible in the early dawn light. There were spaces in the floorboards, and they let in light too, so I burrowed farther into the dark corner, making myself small. I looked down through gaps between my feet. I was directly above the old man's balding scalp.

Could he smell me? I had a moment of panic, but then I realized that my own smell couldn't possibly be stronger than this filthy barn.

The man walked over to the horse's stall and cooed something in German to her. I held my breath. If he looked up, surely he'd see me.

I had an urge to sneeze as he untied her rope. Almost as if we were of one mind, the horse sneezed, spewing snot all over. The farmer chuckled. I looked down and saw that he had darted out of the way just in time. I guess he was used to it.

He led the horse outside and set her loose, walked back into the barn and put a scoop of oats in Beela's trough, then grabbed a pail from a hook on the wall and sat on a stool in her stall. I heard the rhythmic sound of milk drumming the inside of the metal pail. I needed that milk. Not just to soothe my hunger and thirst, but to help heal my festering wound.

The farmer then led Beela outside. I watched through a slat as she ambled over to Kulia, and the two animals munched grass peacefully side by side. The farmer took the pail of milk back with him to the house, and I was hoping that he'd be doing other chores somewhere else and wouldn't notice me. The barn door was still wide open and sunlight shone through. That's when I noticed the branch I'd used as a walking stick down by the cow's trough. Had the farmer seen it?

I waited until he had gone inside the house, then crept back down. I snatched my stick and scrambled back up the stairs.

I had just settled back into my dark corner when the door of the house opened again. A thin woman stepped out. Was she his daughter? Wife?

She walked to the caved-in outbuilding, yanked open a door, and stepped inside. Some time later she came back out, a few chickens following after her. I had been right beside that bombed building and hadn't realized there were live chickens inside!

She now held her basket with both hands. It looked heavy with fresh eggs. My mouth was so dry that my tongue stuck to the roof of it. If I could get one of those eggs, I would crack it over my mouth and swallow it down whole.

I stayed in my hiding spot for the entire day, watching the activity on the farm. When the man used the water pump, it screeched. So much for sneaking out later and getting water. That sound could wake the dead.

The man hitched Kulia to a wagon and went into the muddy field, pulling up turnips and also beets, which I hadn't noticed in the night. I wish I had, because raw beets are much better than turnip. Anything is better than turnip.

It seemed odd that this large farm was being run by just one old man and a frail-looking woman. Where were all the farmhands, or the children? It didn't add up.

While the man harvested, the woman was in and out of the house and other buildings. She brought out a load of laundry and hung trousers and shirts and undergarments on the line. I looked down at my shredded hospital gown.

When the wagon was full, the man led Kulia back to a small building—probably a cold cellar—close to the house. He and the woman unloaded the beets and turnips onto a wheelbarrow and took them inside.

As I watched, my eyes grew heavy and I fell asleep.

CHAPTER FOUR
SNORES

I woke up with a jolt when a bomb hit close by and lit up the night sky. How long had I slept? There was the sound of wheezing directly below me. It was too dark to see, but I knew that Kulia was down there, back in her stall. Why hadn't they done anything about her breathing problem? They only had one horse, after all. The entire situation seemed puzzling.

I tried to stretch out, but my legs were so stiff they felt like they'd break. Gingerly, I felt the filthy stitches in my thigh. The wound was still tender to the touch and I knew it would only get worse if I couldn't clean it. I felt the bottom of my foot where the gash was. The strip of cloth was still wound around it, and it was crusty with mud and blood. It didn't seem to be bleeding anymore and it didn't hurt, but I knew it would take a long time to heal if I kept walking on it. Nothing I could do about that. I had to get away from here as quickly as I could. This farm wasn't very far from the work camp. Someone might come looking for me.

I listed the things I needed to do: clean the stitched-up wound in my thigh, find something to eat, get some clothing and shoes, and get away undetected.

I massaged my legs until I could straighten them. As I slowly climbed down the stairs, Kulia wheezed in greeting. I scratched her muzzle at arm's length to avoid being sprayed with more snot.

Through the darkness I saw the metal milk pail on a wall hook. I grabbed it and limped over to Beela. I had never milked a cow before, but I'd seen Dido do it when he still lived on the *kolkhoz*. I lowered myself down on the wooden stool the farmer had used and placed the pail beneath her.

I found the four teats and gently pulled on the two front ones.

Nothing happened.

Beela stomped a hoof on the floor.

I rubbed my hands together to make sure they were warm, then reached out and gently wrapped my warmed fingers around two of the teats. With gentle pressure, I started at the top and pulled down.

Still nothing.

Then I remembered. The farmer had given Beela some oats before he milked her. I got up and scooped out a cup or so and placed them in her trough. Once she'd begun chewing on her first mouthful, I tried a third time.

A thin trickle of milk hit the bottom of the pail. Slowly, carefully, I milked as Beela chomped on her nighttime snack. I managed to eke out a cup or so. I desperately wanted to grab the pail and tip the contents into my mouth, but I resisted. First I had to clean the wound on my thigh.

I slipped off my filthy hospital gown and found a relatively clean bit of cloth. I dampened it with some of the fresh milk, then gently patted the dirty stitches. Once I'd cleaned it as best I could, I put my gown back on and lifted the pail to my lips. The milk felt like a salve on my parched tongue and throat as I swallowed down every last drop.

"Thank you, Beela. You've saved my life."

With my hunger pangs quiet for the moment and my wounded thigh as clean as it could be, I had to get clothing and footwear and get away from here.

I limped out of the barn and past the ruined chicken coop. Another bomb lit the sky for a flickering moment, giving me a clear flash of the entire house. To my annoyance, the laundry line was empty. I went up to one of the windows and tried to peer through the tar paper but couldn't see anything at all. I had no idea whether the man and woman were awake or sleeping, but given the blackness of the night, it had to be close to midnight. No farmer stayed up that late.

Placing my ear on the front door, I held my breath and listened. At first I heard nothing, but as I filtered away the outdoor sounds, I heard a faint rhythmic noise through the door—the snoring of one person.

In our labor camp, the nights were filled with the sounds of many prisoners trying to sleep—snores, sniffles, weeping, muttering. But this solitary snore brought back memories of safety. Before Tato had been taken, our cozy apartment behind the pharmacy had been filled with a similar sound at night. Sometimes, I had tossed and turned, kept awake by the sawing loudness of it.

"How can you sleep in the same bed with Tato?" I ask Mama. "Don't you get a headache?"

But she just smiles. "I love the sound of your father's snores, Luka. It makes me feel safe."

That first night after he is taken, we sleep on the streets, where the sounds are more terrifying than snores. But David's mother finds us huddled beside the steps of the Grand Hotel on Kreshchatyk Street and takes us home to live with them.

I expect her to take us to their small apartment at the back of the bakery, but I am shocked to see it boarded up. "Not safe there anymore," she says, "what with all the looting."

22

She takes us to where they are living now—a single room they share with the Widow Bilaniuk in a converted mansion.

I fall asleep to the sound of the widow muttering to herself in her dreams, but wake when I hear the muffled weeping of Mama crying into her pillow. That's when I understand about the comforting sound of one person snoring.

I breathed in deeply, burying back the memory. If I could hear snoring through the door, that meant the people inside were asleep. If I could get the door open, I'd be able to quickly take some clothing and boots, and maybe even food if there was something handy. Then I would be on my way.

I turned the doorknob. It was unlocked!

I pushed the door open carefully, trying not to make a sound, but the rusty bolts screeched.

I held my breath. The snoring continued.

Just as I stepped inside the darkness, there was a *click*.

"Hands over your head," said a woman's voice—in German-accented Ukrainian. "Or I'll shoot."

Glaring electric light. A vast sparse kitchen.

Sitting in a carved wooden rocking chair was the woman I'd seen hanging up laundry and collecting eggs. She wore a red bandanna over two thick braids of graying brown hair. Her lips were a grim line of annoyance. She was older than I'd thought and she did not look frail anymore. Her shotgun was pointed at my head.

I raised my hands but scrunched forward. My hospital gown was quite short, and I didn't want to embarrass myself.

Her gaze took in my appearance from head to toe. Her nose wrinkled. "You are a filthy thief."

Her accent reminded me of the wardens at the work camp. They spoke Ukrainian, Russian, or Polish, but always with that heavy German sound to it. The snoring in the next room stopped.

"Margarete, are you all right?" a man's voice asked in German.

"It's under control, Helmut."

Moments later the old man came into the room, buttoning his red flannel shirt, his feet bare and his hair awry.

"He's a scrawny one," Helmut said. "How old do you think he is? Twelve?" He must not have realized that I could understand him. Or maybe he just didn't care. "Are you going to shoot him, or do you want me to?"

"Please don't shoot!" I said in German.

The man seemed surprised that I could speak a bit of his language, and that made him hesitate for a minute. But then he said, "You may be just a child, but you tramp through my field, break into my barn, and disrupt the animals—muddy footprints all over the place—and now you come into our *house*."

What would he have done in my place? Anger boiled up inside me, but I forced myself to look calm. I hung my head in what I hoped looked like contrition. "I am sorry for the damage I've caused to your property."

The man snorted.

"Why didn't you just knock?" asked Margarete, again in Ukrainian. She'd lowered the shotgun, but her finger still touched the trigger and she had the gun directed vaguely toward my chest.

Was she serious? An escapee from the local slave-labor camp should just saunter up to a German farmhouse and knock on the door, asking for help?

"Would you have helped me if I had done that?"

The woman shrugged. "Maybe. You're not the first one to escape."

"But you might also have turned me in. Or shot me."

"So instead, you become a thief," Margarete muttered.

"I am unarmed, injured, and hungry," I shot back. "Call me a thief if you wish. I was just going to take clothing and shoes, maybe something to eat."

"Does this farm look prosperous to you?"

I didn't reply.

"Do you think we *want* to be in this godforsaken place? We were dumped here."

All at once, it made sense. No wonder they could speak Ukrainian. We had German neighbors in Kyiv before the war, but they disappeared in 1939. I had assumed they'd all ended up in Siberia or in the mass graves. Some of them had, I am sure. But during those first two years of the war when Hitler and Stalin were on the same side, a lot of people had to move.

"The Nazis gave us this farm," said Margarete. "But we have no help and almost no livestock. And our sons have been forced into the army."

I put on a sympathetic face for Margarete, but I couldn't muster much compassion for her. It made me wonder who had lived at this farm before, and where *they* were right now.

And I also had been taken from my home by the Nazis, but unlike this German couple, I hadn't exactly been given a farm. Lida had been taken from her home too, and had lost her entire family. Like me, she was forced to work twelve hours a day for the Germans, surviving on nothing but a thin gruel of turnip soup. She wasn't the only one. In my camp, there were thousands. How many slave-labor camps were there? How many of those workers would have thought they were in heaven to be at a farm like this? But

I couldn't say that to these people. They wouldn't understand.

"You are not starving" was all I said.

She looked over at her husband. It was as if they were having a silent conversation. He nodded slightly. She lowered the gun.

"I don't know if we can trust you," said Margarete. "But we'll hold off on shooting you until we decide. First, let's get you cleaned up."

CHAPTER FIVE
EGGS

Perhaps the farm was not prosperous at the moment, but when Helmut led me to their bathroom, I was stunned. A huge porcelain tub on big clawed feet, a real flush toilet, and a gleaming white pedestal sink. It was hard to believe that this fancy bathroom was for just a single family. The people who lived here before the war had certainly been well off.

"That rag you're wearing"—Helmut held out a wastebasket—"throw it in."

As I stood there naked, embarrassed, and cold, I watched him adjust the faucets until water came out of the showerhead. He set a sponge and bar of soap on a wire shelf above the taps and pulled a thick curtain around the tub to keep the water from spraying about—that was something I had never seen before. He draped a towel over the sink for me and hung a nightshirt on the hook at the back of the door. Then he left.

I climbed into the shower, my thigh protesting when I lifted it over the high edge of the tub. Warm water rained down through my hair and face and over my body. Black streaks swirled down the drain. As the layers of dirt came off, I began to feel more human. I thought of Lida, still in that horrible work camp, and me, powerless to help her. My mother, lost. And Tato too. But they were probably still alive. And then I thought of David. In the end, he was killed and I still lived. What kind of friend was I?

Whatever this couple was up to, my plan remained the same: get clothing, food, shoes, then leave. I had to survive this war, find my parents—Tato first—then get back to Lida and take her home with me. I couldn't help David anymore, but I would not abandon Lida.

I dried off, my skin pale without the grime. Now that my leg injury was clean, I could see that the milk wash had done its job. The stitches no longer strained and the skin was less swollen and red. I sat at the side of the tub to examine the wound on my foot. It had been a deep puncture, but it was beginning to heal. My makeshift first aid had helped.

I got into the nightshirt. It was old, but the flannel was

good quality. If I couldn't find trousers to steal, this shirt would do.

When I stepped out of the bathroom, Helmut was there, waiting for me. He blinked when he saw me. "For a moment there, you looked like Claus," he said, pointing to the nightshirt.

"Claus?"

"My younger son."

"Where is he now?"

"The Eastern Front," he said grimly. "I pray that he doesn't end up fighting in our old home village."

"I hope he doesn't end up in Kyiv. That's where I'm from," I said. Did Helmut realize what his son might be up to on the Eastern Front? The nightshirt suddenly felt like it was going to strangle me. I undid the top button and took a deep breath.

"From Kyiv, are you?" he said. "A long way from here. What's your name?"

Should I tell him my real name, or make one up? They hadn't shot me and they'd been kind so far, so I decided to return the courtesy and tell them the truth. "My name is Luka Barukovich."

Helmut took my hand and shook it firmly, then turned, motioning me to follow him. I limped behind him, back to the huge kitchen. "Sit," he said, pointing to one of the kitchen chairs. "Show me your foot."

He sat on a low stool like the one he milked Beela with, set a pair of glasses on the end of his nose, and examined the cut. "It's not infected," he said, looking over the lenses at me. "A surprise, considering how filthy you were."

He got up and rooted around in the cupboards, then sat back down on the stool, holding a bottle of iodine, plus scissors, tape, and gauze. I didn't flinch when he put a few stinging drops of the iodine into the wound. He wrapped the gauze around my foot.

Next he examined the wound on my thigh. "This seems to be healing well," he said. "How did you manage to keep it clean?"

"Milk," I said. "From your cow."

Helmut's eyebrows raised slightly at this piece of information, but he didn't respond.

During all of this, I watched Margarete from the corner of my eye. She sat silently at her spot at the opposite end of the table. At first I thought she was watching me, but when I had a chance to turn and actually look, I realized that I was probably the last thing on her mind. She seemed utterly lost in thought. At least she'd put the shotgun away.

"Why don't you make the boy something to eat?" Helmut said as he stood up from the stool. "I'm going back to bed."

Margarete jerked as if she'd been woken from a deep sleep. She nodded to Helmut, then focused on me. "Eggs?"

Eggs! How long had it been? "Thank you for your kindness," I replied.

She stood up and smoothed the front of her dress, then walked over to the gas range. Before the war, this kitchen must have fed an entire family and the field hands as well. Margarete took a giant skillet and cracked in two eggs. I licked my lips when she added a dollop of butter. When was the last time I had tasted butter?

As the scent of sizzling eggs filled the kitchen, she glanced at me over her shoulder. "You are probably thirsty," she said. "Get yourself some milk from the icebox. Glasses are over there." She indicated an oversized cupboard.

This woman was a puzzle. She'd just as soon feed me as shoot me.

In addition to the pitcher of milk, there was cheese and a sausage, some apples, two pears, and a jar of strawberry preserves in the icebox. My fingers itched. I would steal some of this when I made my escape.

When Margarete put the scrambled eggs in front of me, I was so hungry I felt like shoveling them into my mouth, but I didn't want to be rude. I filled my fork and took the first mouthful, loving the taste. But when I brought the second forkful to my lips, I paused. People that I knew and loved were starving. Others had already died. It seemed criminal to be enjoying a meal like this.

In my mind, I saw Lida sitting across from me, having her thin turnip soup and sawdust bread at the slave-labor camp. Her image dissolved and David's appeared—mischievous smile and all. How often had we scoured the streets of Kyiv together in search of food? He would have loved this meal.

Margarete methodically wiped the long counter with a damp rag. "Is there something the matter with the eggs?"

"They are delicious," I managed to say.

I took a deep breath and pushed the sadness to the back of my mind. I couldn't bring David back to life, and Lida would want me to eat. Hadn't I promised to find her after the war? I could keep that promise only if I stayed strong. I took another mouthful of egg. Soon, Margarete would be asleep. I'd get food, find a pair of shoes, maybe some trousers, and be on my way.

But once I finished eating, Margarete took me down a long, dark hallway. It was surprising how big the house was, considering how plain it looked from the outside.

She opened a door and switched on an electric light.

This room held a sturdy four-poster bed covered with a feather duvet, a bookshelf, and a wardrobe.

"This was Martin's room," she said. "Have a good night."

"You want me to sleep in this room?" I had assumed I'd be sleeping back in the barn or out with the chickens.

"You've got to sleep somewhere," she said. Her voice was flat, emotionless.

I stepped into the bedroom and she walked out. As she closed the door, I heard a bolt click from the outside.

CHAPTER SIX
TRAPPED

I stood there, at a loss. So much for my plan of a quick escape.

I walked to the window. There was no glass left in it at all. It was covered with a latticework of wood and tar-papered on the outside so no light could get through. I tried to open the window, but it was nailed closed. Had they locked others in this room before me? What did these people want?

I sat on the edge of the bed, but I was not tired. I needed to figure out how to escape. I went over to the shelf and sat on the rug so I could see the books. There was an oversized world atlas angled sideways on the bottom shelf. I took it out and opened it. The publishing date was 1935—before the Nazi-Soviet alliance that carved up Eastern Europe.

I turned the pages until I found a map of what had been the Soviet Union back then. Kyiv was easy to find. I placed my finger over it and closed my eyes, wishing I were there. I tried to find a page that showed Kyiv and Germany on the same map so I could figure out how far away I was from home, but Germany was too big. I knew I had to be somewhere close to the Alps, which were attached to the Carpathians—but where? There was a city sign for Breslau on the road outside the camp, but I couldn't find Breslau on this map. Maybe Helmut or Margarete would tell me where we were.

The middle shelf held books of various shapes and sizes. I pulled one out. On the cover was a painting of an American Indian holding a shotgun. He had a red bandanna around his brow and braids hanging down over his shoulders. For a moment I was reminded of Margarete. I slid the book back into its spot and pulled out another. This one showed a girl standing in front of a mountain range. She looked like a well-fed Lida.

The top shelf was crammed with books that looked like they had been read often, with spines bent and curling bookmarks sticking out from the pages. Each book had a swastika symbol stamped on the spine. I couldn't read German well enough to figure out all of the titles, but one I had heard of before—*Mein Kampf* by Adolf Hitler. This was the book that turned some people into Nazis—making them think they were a better kind of human than anyone else. The very sight of it made me want to throw up.

I stood and walked over to the wardrobe. When I opened it, I was enveloped in the unpleasant bleach-ammonia smell of mothballs. Inside was a narrow shelf with neat stacks of folded clothing to one side, and what looked like a grayish-green suit on a hanger in the main part. When I pulled the suit out to get a better look, I nearly dropped it. On the collar was the distinctive Death's Head insignia. This was an SS officer's uniform. Was this a spare uniform of Martin's? I would never steal this to wear. Better to go naked. I hung up the uniform and pushed the wardrobe shut.

I turned the light switch off, flopped onto the bed, and closed my eyes—just for a moment, just to rest them. I had to think of a way out of this situation. These farm people seemed kind, but their son was a Nazi. How could I trust them?

As I lay on the soft bed, my mind drifted back to another soft bed and another encounter with Germans.

I am stretched out on the bare mattress in a corner of the room that we share with David Kagan, his mother, and the Widow Bilaniuk. Bright sun shines through the window. The first thing I notice is absolute silence. No bombs, explosions, or bullets. For days the outdoor speakers have announced, "Kyiv was, is, and will be Soviet." Over and over and over. But now the speakers are silent.

I join David at the window. Down below, crowds line the streets. From a distance, I hear a tinny loudspeaker. As the sound gets closer, we hear an announcement in German-accented Russian: "Kyiv is now in German hands. You have been liberated from the Soviets."

A Nazi army truck slowly rolls by. On its roof is the loud-speaker. In the back of the truck are German soldiers. They are not holding weapons. They are smiling and waving. Behind them march rows and rows of more soldiers.

David and I run outside and stand on the sidewalk to get a better look. We aren't the only ones—the streets are crowded with confused and silent people. Some balconies have been deco-rated with flowers.

Now that I am closer, I marvel at these clean-faced, smiling soldiers. Their uniforms are not tattered like the Soviet ones, and their leather boots shine. They do not seem to be the devils that Stalin told us they were.

People in the crowd have no idea how to behave. A girl beside me waves timidly, and one of the younger soldiers stops to shake her hand. An old woman approaches him and thrusts a bouquet of flowers into his hands. Everyone around me stops talking, stops breathing, as if they are waiting for something to happen.

The soldier smiles. He reaches into his pocket. For a gun?

But he pulls out a little phrase book and says in tortured Russian, "Thank you."

A collective sigh of relief. Maybe it will be better now. Maybe the killing will stop. Tato told me that for hundreds of years, Germans and Ukrainians had developed good relations. But it doesn't feel right to cheer the defeat of our own government. I turn to David, and he looks as puzzled and somber as the rest of the crowd . . .

I wanted to think of that time—maybe it would help me puzzle out what was happening now. But before I knew it, I fell asleep.

When I opened my eyes the next morning, a few narrow slits of sunlight had managed to shine through the cracks in the tar paper. It took me a moment to remember that I was at a farm with a strangely friendly German couple. I tried to open the door, but it was still locked. I walked over to the window, poked my finger through some of the tar paper, and peeked through. Beela and Kulia were already grazing outside the barn. It was later than I had imagined.

Moments later the bolt slid back and the door opened. Margarete stood there with a pair of work trousers and a faded green flannel shirt.

"I found these for you," she said, handing them to me. "You wouldn't want to wear anything from this room." Her eyes drifted over to the wardrobe. "These," she said, resting a finger on the fabric, "may be old, but they are honest working clothes."

Her comments relieved me. Martin might be her son, but she was not proud of him.

"Come to the kitchen for something to eat once you're dressed," she said. "And then we'll figure out what we'll do with you."

When I stepped into the kitchen, I could smell potato pancakes sizzling in bacon fat. Helmut was already sitting at the table with a cup of coffee. A book was open in front of him. He looked up at me and said in Ukrainian, "Good morning."

I wished him the same, then walked over to the cooking range where Margarete stood, frying up the last of the pancakes.

"Is there something I can do to help you?" I asked.

"Go into the pantry and get us some honey," she said, pointing to a double set of doors in the wall close to the icebox.

Like everything else in this farmhouse, the storage area was massive. All sorts of food lined the shelves—tins of tea, coffee substitute, and powdered chocolate, but no tin of honey. Burlap sacks sat neatly lined up on the bottom shelves, labeled in various languages—it had to be booty from the war. Rice, barley, flour—these I could decipher, but it was hard to know what every item was.

I stepped out of the pantry. "I cannot find the honey," I said to Margarete.

"Look in the white cloth sack on the top shelf."

When I looked back into the pantry, I could only see one white cloth bag and it had *Muka*—"Flour"—stamped on the outside. I pulled it down from the shelf and untied it. Inside were coils of what looked like linked sausages, but the contents were nearly translucent. I rooted around until I found a single sausage that wasn't attached to the rest and brought it out.

"Thank you," said Margarete, taking it from me.

I watched as she slit the top of the sausage casing and squeezed the contents into a small jar. "Claus sent this," she said. "From the Eastern Front. We used to keep bees ourselves when we lived in Bukovyna."

That comment made me so angry. When the Soviets retreated from the Nazis in 1941, they left us civilians with nothing. These coils of honey hidden in sausage casings might have kept an entire family alive on the Eastern Front, but for this man, Claus, it was just war booty.

Margarete looked at me oddly, perhaps understanding the anger I felt. "Sit," she said. "I know you're hungry." She set a small plate of crispy pancakes in front of me. "I would give you more," she said, "but your stomach is not used to rich and plentiful food."

I cut a small piece of pancake and put it into my mouth. The anger slowly evaporated as I chewed. Helmut and Margarete ate their breakfasts silently, pretending to ignore me, but once I saw Helmut glance up at me and frown. I ate every crumb on my plate. I felt like lifting the plate up to my face and licking it, to get every last bit, but I resisted. My stomach felt like it would burst.

After the meal, Margarete took down two more cups and filled them with coffee. Without asking, she stirred a big spoonful of honey into the one for me. "We need to talk."

I took a sip from the cup and looked at her.

"We will give you what you wanted to steal," she said. "The weather will be getting cold soon, and it's always raining around here, so I'll need to find you something to use as a groundsheet."

"You'll want food that's easy to carry," said Helmut. "And sturdy footwear."

"Thank you," I said, taken aback by their words. Why were they being so helpful? Was this some sort of trick, or were they simply good people?

"But what I want to know," said Margarete, "is where do you think you can go?"

If I told them my dream was to get back to Kyiv and find my father, would they think I was crazy? My short-term plan wasn't much more than staying alive until the war ended. I could head to the mountains and get away from the Germans. If Tato survived, he'd certainly go back to Kyiv. Then together we'd find Mama—and Lida. My eyes met Margarete's and I could see her concern.

"I've survived by hiding," I said. "Maybe I'll keep on doing that."

Helmut tapped the kitchen table with a coffee spoon. "You are lucky that you ended up on our farm and not somewhere else."

"I don't want to overstay my welcome," I said. What I really meant was that I wanted to leave as soon as I could.

"Helmut," said Margarete, "the boy cannot leave right now. How far do you think he'd get on that foot? And that wound on his thigh—it's not fully healed."

"It's fine," I said. "I can walk."

They ignored my words.

"So you think it's worth the risk to let him stay here for a while to regain his strength?" asked Helmut.

"If he leaves now, he's almost certain to die. If he stays and is caught, he will die." Margarete took a slow sip from her cup.

"So our only choice is to hide him and hope he doesn't get caught."

"We'll put some fat on his bones and give him time to heal up," said Margarete. "Then he'll have a fighting chance to survive on the run."

It felt odd to have them talking about me as if I weren't there. My stomach gurgled from too much food.

Helmut turned to me and said, "Someone could see you from a distance."

"He'll have to stay inside," said Margarete.

CHAPTER SEVEN
MOUNTAINS

The thought of staying in a warm house with plenty of food and hot running water didn't seem like it would be a hardship, but after a few days of inactivity, I was desperate for something to do. I had peeled back a bit more of the tar paper from Martin's bedroom window, and from one angle I could see the mountains in the distance. I wanted to get to those mountains. Their treacherous landscape would stop an army, but not one person. They would keep me safe.

In the meantime, I stuffed myself. Each morning Margarete would cook up eggs, or potato pancakes, or if there were leftovers from the previous night's dinner, we'd have that instead. Beef and dumplings for breakfast? An incredible treat. When I looked in the bathroom mirror, I could see that I was filling out.

But was their generosity too good to be true? The friendliness of the Germans who took over Kyiv had only been skin-deep—I knew that too well. Would Helmut and Margarete change, the way those other Germans had? The quicker I was away from here, the better. Otherwise, I would become as soft as Martin's bed.

On the sixth morning, while Helmut applied the daily coating of iodine to the wound on my foot, he said, "It's almost healed." A week later, he removed the stitches in my thigh. Soon I would be strong enough to leave.

"Whatever gave you the idea to put *milk* on this?" He shook his head as he pulled out the last stitch with tweezers. "You Slavs sure are backward."

"My father is a pharmacist."

"And your father taught you to put milk on an infected wound?"

"It is a traditional remedy."

He shook his head. "Slavs . . ."

"The Soviets destroyed all of his medications before they evacuated Kyiv."

"An old tactic: Leave nothing behind that can be used by the enemy."

Or by the civilians who are abandoned by their own government, I thought, but didn't say.

Helmut wrinkled his brow. "What other things did your father teach you to use?"

"Things from around here, you mean?" I asked. "A piece of moldy bread, honey."

Helmut looked skeptical.

I smiled. "Often what we need to survive is right at our fingertips."

Helmut looked up. "Anything at our fingertips to make Blitz healthy again?"

"Blitz?"

"The horse."

I had gotten so used to thinking of her as Kulia that I'd forgotten it was only my name for her. "Can't you get a veterinarian?"

"They're all in the army. Their medicines too," Helmut said.

"My father showed me a way to treat wheezing in humans," I said. "It may work for your horse."

"No milk washes for my Blitz," said Helmut.

"A bit of honey in her drinking water—and it should be warmed up—that will loosen the mucus."

"Well, I suppose it won't hurt," said Helmut. "And we have lots of honey."

After dark, I took a pail of warmed honey water into

the barn for Blitz. Then I helped Helmut carry in a laundry tub full of steaming water. I placed a blanket over Blitz's head to form a sort of steam tent.

Almost right away, Blitz began to breathe more easily.

Helmut and Margarete didn't lock me in at night anymore, so I would go out and visit the animals. It felt good just to be there in the barn with them, leaning into their warmth and feeling the rhythm of their breathing. Even with bombs still exploding outside, I felt safe.

After a few days the weather turned mild, and I took a wheelbarrow out to the fields in the cover of night to dig up turnips for Helmut. My back ached from filling just a single load. How did an old man like him manage this alone?

As safe as I felt with Helmut and Margarete, though, I was anxious to get going. My foot was fully healed as far as I could tell, and my leg no longer gave me trouble.

One evening after dinner, Margarete set a small plate of ginger cookies on the table and served each of us a glass of hot tea. I took a sip as I considered how kindly they had treated me. In many ways I would miss them.

"Helmut, Margarete," I said, setting down my glass. "Thank you for all that you have done for me, but it is time for me to leave."

"You are welcome to stay here," she said.

Her words were not a surprise. I had sensed that she enjoyed having a bit more company. "I'm putting you both in danger."

"But this is the worst time of year to travel," said Margarete. "It rains nearly every day. Soon it will be December. To be traveling in the snow is almost as difficult. How can you hide? How can you stay warm?"

"And where would you go?" asked Helmut.

"To the mountains."

Helmut blinked in surprise. "Do you even know where you are?" he asked.

"Somewhere in Germany . . ." I thought of the atlas on the bookshelf in Martin's bedroom. "Just a minute . . ."

I retrieved the atlas from the bedroom and flipped it open to a page I had studied so many times.

"Can you show me where we are?" I asked.

Helmut got up from his chair and stood beside me. He rested one hand on my shoulder and frowned as he examined the page. "Where do you think we are?"

One German city I recognized was München—Munich. I put my finger on it. "Are we close to here?"

"No." Helmut placed his finger on a spot that was on the other side of Czechoslovakia. "We are in a rural area close to Breslau."

"But the atlas says Wroclaw, and it's in *Poland,* not Germany."

"It's part of the Reich now. The name was changed."

"But all the people around here are German, not Polish. And the signs—everything is German."

Helmut stared at me in surprise. "I told you—Margarete and I are not from around here."

I nodded. But I still didn't really understand.

"When Hitler and Stalin were on the same side between 1939 and 1941," said Helmut, "they carved up Poland between them. Hitler wanted Germans in his part of Poland and Stalin wanted Slavs. People were moved. Hundreds of thousands of us. On both sides."

"And without any warning either," said Margarete. "They shipped out all of the Germans in our town. We were sent to a holding camp to be evacuated—and we were the lucky ones. Some were shipped to labor camps. Some went to Germany. Our family was sent here."

"What about the people who were here before?"

"The Poles? They were taken away. We replaced them."

Helmut nodded. "We got to this house, and there was still food on the table. Children's clothing was scattered on the floor in Martin's bedroom."

"What happened to them? The Polish families?" I asked.

Margarete looked away. "They were sent to the Soviet Union."

A flash of memory—*That grave in the forest overflowing with corpses. A bit of paper written in Polish script fluttering out of a dead woman's coat* . . . I knew what might have happened to the families. They certainly weren't given the newly vacated German homes.

"Those mountains in the distance," I said. "Are those linked to the Carpathians?"

Helmut slowly turned the pages of the atlas. "This map shows it better."

He angled the book so I could see the map more easily. "Here we are, and here are those mountains." He pointed to a hook-shaped cluster of mountains farther south and east. "The ones we see in the distance—to the southeast? They're on the western edge of the Carpathians."

"I need to get there," I said.

"But they're hundreds of kilometers away," said Margarete.

"And you'd be hunted down long before you got there," Helmut added.

"I need to try."

"Stay here until the spring," said Helmut. "The weather will be kinder. You'll be stronger."

They looked at me in silence. The clock above the mantel ticked.

Then a car horn blared outside and Margarete jumped up so quickly her chair toppled over. "Martin! Home for a visit." She ran over and pushed me toward the pantry. "Hide!"

CHAPTER EIGHT
MARTIN

The pantry door closed, plunging me into darkness. I stood, not daring to breathe. Sounds trickled through—a chair set upright, tea splashed into the sink, the squeak of the kitchen door, the rustling of a paper bag.

A man's voice said, "Mutti, Vati, it's so good to see you. This is for you."

That voice. It sounded so familiar. Where . . . ? No, it couldn't be . . . !

I knew I was taking a risk, but I opened the pantry door just a crack to see if I was right.

My heart stopped. Standing there with a paper bag in one hand, hugging Margarete and Helmut, was Officer Schmidt from my labor camp! Strutting, power-hungry Officer Schmidt. *This* man was their son Martin?

I sneaked the door closed. I was plunged once more into darkness.

My knees felt weak and I grabbed a shelf. All these days that I had been fattening myself up and letting my wounds heal, I had been sleeping in the bed of a monster. This same man had selected young children in our camp to be killed, others to be worked to death. And he had seemed to enjoy it. How could gentle people like Margarete and Helmut have raised to someone like him?

If he caught me, he would shoot me. At least Margarete and Helmut would not be in danger—not from their own son. Would they? I lowered myself to the floor of the pantry. Using my hands to gauge what was around me, I cleared a spot in the back corner and shuffled into it. I pulled a burlap sack of rice in front of myself.

The pantry door was still open a crack, so even from my hiding spot in the back, I could hear the conversation.

"Sit down, son," said Helmut, in a voice that to me sounded falsely hearty. "Mutti and I were just having a glass of tea. Would you like some too?"

"I've brought you some freshly baked cherry buns," said Martin. There was the rustle of a bag being ripped open. "What about some of that cherry vodka I brought you last time? The two would go together nicely."

"I'll get it," said Helmut.

Suddenly the pantry filled with light. Helmut walked in and grabbed a bottle from a high shelf at the front. His face looked pale and tense, but when he caught my eye and saw me somewhat hidden, his shoulders relaxed. He backed out and I was plunged again into darkness.

Cupboards squeaked open and glasses tinkled. Chairs scraped along the floor. I figured they were all sitting around the table, sipping vodka and nibbling fresh buns.

"Will you be staying the night?" Margarete asked.

"I must get back to the camp. I was just on my way back from town and had a moment to drive by. We've had some problems."

"Problems?"

"The munitions factory was bombed a few weeks back. A lot of our laborers were there. Many killed. Many more wounded. That's not the bad part—such things happen in war. But one escaped from the hospital, and that's given the other prisoners ideas."

"I am sure it will blow over," said Margarete.

"I hope so, Mutti," Martin replied. "But I can't be gone too long."

There was the sound of a long sip and then the clatter of a glass being put down on the table with a bit too much force. "To make matters worse, we're getting new shipments every day. The Soviets are closing in and the eastern camps are being evacuated. We're getting their prisoners."

"Then you have more help in the munitions plant," said Helmut.

"These new ones are worthless," said Martin. "They're starved to the point of death. I can't use them."

I clenched my fists. These were living, breathing humans he was talking about.

The sound of liquid tinkling into a glass. "You've got my old atlas out," said Officer Schmidt. "What a relic that is."

"Yes," said Margarete. "We were just saying the same to each other. The Reich has certainly expanded."

"I wish it were still expanding," said Officer Schmidt. "These are darker days. Any letters from Claus?"

"No," said Helmut. "We're worried. Have you heard anything?"

"Not directly," said Officer Schmidt. "But I've had word that the Soviets recaptured Kyiv just a few days ago."

"Was there much to recapture?" asked Helmut.

Helmut was probably being wily, asking this question for me.

"Next to nothing. We succeeded in starving out the city before it was recaptured."

I felt like punching something. Kyiv destroyed, and here I was, hiding out in the enemy's house. I had to get out of here. I had to fight. Exactly how or with what, I had no idea.

Martin stayed and drank and talked for a while longer. It was getting so late that I was sure he would decide to stay over, but then his chair scraped back on the kitchen floor.

"I need to be going," he said. "It's been so good to visit with you, Mutti, Vati."

The sound of squeaking hinges, then the pantry doors shook slightly from a gust of wind. Grunts of exertion and heavy footsteps, then a large object being dragged across the floor.

"Do you want me to put these things into the pantry for you before I go?" Martin asked.

I held my breath.

"No," said Margarete. I caught the nervous catch in her voice. I hoped Officer Schmidt would not. "You must be on your way. And I need to sort it all out before I put it away."

Moments after Officer Schmidt left, light flooded into the pantry. I got to my feet. A bag sat in the middle of the table, cherry buns spilling out of it.

On the floor between the pantry and the table was a large burlap sack. I was still trying to digest the fact that Officer Schmidt had been mere inches away from me.

"I want to leave *right now*."

"Sit down and listen to us," said Margarete.

I slumped down in the chair. Why hadn't they told me who their son was?

"We haven't seen Martin for a while," said Helmut. "We are not on good terms."

"You seemed on good terms to me."

Margarete went into another room, coming back moments later with a photo album. She set it in front of me and opened it to one of the more recent pages. "This is a picture of our two sons," she said. "While they were still innocent."

I recognized Martin immediately. His shoulders were thrown back and his head held high. In contrast, Claus had an easy smile.

"Martin had no choice, really," said Margarete. "We had to prove our loyalty to the Reich. Claus enlisted right away. Martin didn't want to. The SS came for him and gave him a choice: Work with them or send us to the work camp."

"Sadly, he became good at his new job," added Helmut bitterly. "We cannot believe how much he has changed. They promoted him quickly."

Margarete took a deep breath. "He brought us forced workers. We told him we wouldn't take people who are treated like slaves. We're not barbarians. But he said we had to take them, or our loyalty would be questioned."

"*His* loyalty too," said Helmut.

"So we took six," said Margarete.

"And they all escaped," said Helmut.

"He got into trouble," said Helmut. "And that changed him."

I had to think carefully of what to say next. "Thank you for protecting me, for saving my life. But now I need to leave. To get to the mountains. Can you help me?"

Helmut got up from the table and came back with a pencil and paper. I watched as he sketched a map, added Xs all over one area, then roads, railway tracks, a river, woods, the beginning of mountains.

"We're here," he said, resting the tip of his pencil on one corner of the paper that was covered with Xs and was far away from the mountains. "This part"—his index finger swept over the area of road and railway—"is very dangerous for you. We need to get you past all of this and to the forested areas along the Oder River."

Margarete nodded. "We've done it before. If you follow the Oder River south, you'll get to the foothills of the mountains."

"But you must be careful," said Helmut. "Specially trained soldiers patrol the forested areas, looking for people like you. And the Oder River is used for military transport, so you'll need to stay hidden."

I knew it would be dangerous, but I was eager to start the journey. "When can you take me?"

"Tomorrow morning, first thing. That would be best," said Margarete.

"Thank you," I said again. These two had been so kind and now they were risking their lives for me—a stranger who had tried to steal from them.

Margarete got up from the table and walked over to the burlap bag that Martin had left. "Maybe it was good that our son visited us after all," she said. "I'm sure something in here will come in handy for you."

CHAPTER NINE
OBERSTURMBANNFÜHRER PFAFF

I went to bed, but could not sleep. Now that I knew Officer Schmidt had slept in these sheets, I felt the weight of them like chains.

I closed my eyes.

An image of Lida appears, her eyes wide with terror. It's the same expression as when we first met. She is the last captured child to be thrown into the back of our truck heading for a slave-labor camp in the Reich. Most of the children weep with fear, but not Lida. Instead, she does her best to calm the others and to give us all hope: She gets us to sing. That's what I love the most about Lida—this gift she has of finding goodness in even the worst situations.

I pulled the covers up to my chin and tried to get some sleep, but the memory of Lida would not leave me alone. Now she appeared as I had last seen her on the day before I escaped. She'd sneaked into my hospital room and woken me up. "I want you out of this place," she'd whispered fiercely. Without her blessing, I would never have escaped. What had she known that I didn't?

I covered my face with my hands and tried to banish all thoughts. I had to be rested for tomorrow. I fell into an uneasy sleep.

A light tapping startled me awake. Margarete opened the bedroom door, and the brightness of the electric light in the hallway made me squint. She held a dress.

"Get washed up and put these on," she said. "I've packed some food. We'll eat in the wagon."

"Should I put this on over my other clothes?"

"No. It would be too bulky. I'll pack up your regular clothing." Margarete's eyes lit up and she smiled. "In that sack that Martin brought, there were ten American army rations—small boxed meals. I've packed them all for you."

"Thank you."

Margarete grabbed me in a hug. "Stay safe," she whispered. "I could never forgive myself if something happened to you."

I closed my eyes, and for a moment it was almost like hugging Mama . . .

She reaches out for me one last time. "May your wits keep you safe, my son," she cries. And then a Nazi soldier smashes her head with a club and she tumbles to the ground. He picks her up like a rag doll and throws her into the boxcar.

I pulled loose from Margarete and took a deep breath. She left without another word.

What I thought was a dress was actually two pieces. I pulled on the skirt part and tried doing up the blouse, but the buttons were on the wrong side. Didn't that bother girls? As I walked into the bathroom, the skirt material got caught around my legs.

I looked at myself in the mirror. Putting on a skirt and a blouse did not make me look like a girl. It made me look like a boy in a skirt.

"Can I come in?" said Margarete through the bathroom door.

I opened it. "This isn't going to fool anyone."

She looked at me and stifled a laugh. Anger surged up inside me. The skirt was embarrassing enough, but she didn't have to laugh. A good disguise could be a matter of life and death.

She pulled a kerchief out of her pocket. "Face the mirror," she said. "I've got to get this right."

I watched as she folded the cloth sideways to make a large triangle and then put it on my head. She pulled it tightly from the back, then tied all three corners of the kerchief together.

She drew a small cotton bundle from her pocket. Unwrapping a corner, she showed me one of last night's cherry buns. She closed the cloth over the bun, then tucked it inside the back of my kerchief until it was snug against the nape of my neck, like long hair coiled up under the kerchief.

I stared in the mirror. The person looking out was no longer me. The image was eerily like my own mother.

"Take small steps. I think we can pass you off as a farm girl."

When we got outside, it was still dark. Helmut had strapped Blitz into her harness, and the wagon was filled with sacks of turnip.

"Normally we'd be making a delivery sometime this week," he said as he took Margarete's hand and helped her up to the wooden bench at the front of the wagon. "Get up on the other side, Luka."

I hoisted myself up and sat beside Margarete, but Helmut stayed where he was, a pensive look on his face.

"Your knapsack is packed," he said. "It's under the bench, at your feet."

"Aren't you coming too?"

He shook his head. "It would be suspicious. With you and Margarete, it will look like I was sick and so you're here to help. Which reminds me . . ." He reached into the pocket on the inside of his jacket and drew out what looked like a small gray booklet. He thrust it into my hand.

The outside was embossed with the Reich logo of a swastika in a circle, and an eagle with outspread wings above. Identity papers. Something I did not have. I opened it. Official stamps. The photograph of a woman who looked something like Margarete, only younger. In the spot for a name, it said *Berta Pfaff.*

"She was my niece," said Margarete. "She had been sickly for a long time and died last year, but I managed to keep her papers, and they've come in handy more than once. If we're stopped along the way, hopefully the soldiers won't look at them too carefully."

Helmut reached up and clasped my hand in a firm shake. "Stay safe, Luka."

I would miss Margarete and Helmut. "I am grateful for your many kindnesses."

Margarete flicked her whip lightly on Blitz's rump.

Blitz didn't sneeze or wheeze, but she groaned as she leaned into the harness. As we slowly rode down the farm drive in the darkness of early morning, I watched the silhouette of the buildings that had saved my life. A bomb exploded in the distance, and for one brief moment I saw Helmut standing there, his hand raised in a wave goodbye. I waved back.

Margarete and I traveled many kilometers, bouncing up and down on the wooden bench. Sometimes I gripped with both hands to keep from falling off. Once, a front wheel plunged into a deep crater and we both lurched forward. Blitz grunted and pulled, but we were stuck. I got out and pushed on the wheel with my shoulder while Blitz strained forward. Finally the wheel moved. I climbed back onto the bench, dusting dirt from my hands and clothing.

"I know you had to get the wagon going again," said Margarete, dabbing some dirt from my cheek with a handkerchief. "But now you look like a boy in a skirt. Try to compose yourself. Knees together, elbows in, and let me get you clean."

The sun rose as we got closer to town and I gazed at the strip of mountains in the distance. Would I really be able to get to them? I had to try, no matter what.

Once we turned off the main road, we stopped briefly for tea and buns.

I took a swig of tea, then passed the flask to Margarete. As I bit into a cherry bun from my knapsack, my mind filled with the memory of David and the special breads his father would make. I chewed slowly, thinking of him.

We rode together in silence for some time. We passed a wagon going in the opposite direction and Margarete nodded in greeting but didn't slow down. Once, a military truck sped past us, in a hurry to get somewhere. It was broad daylight now and unseasonably warm. From where I sat on the wagon bench, I could see the area that surrounded us. Mostly farms, with fields and buildings pockmarked with damage from Allied attacks.

Margarete turned south onto a smaller road and we traveled in silence through a small hamlet with half a dozen bombed-out houses in a cluster. There were no people here. Had they been evacuated before the bombs hit? She turned onto another road, this one heading east. We kept on going in silence, not meeting anyone at all, and not seeing any more houses.

Just when I relaxed slightly, we encountered a German army truck idling at the side of the road. A soldier was sprawled across the hood, immersed in a book. A second soldier was in the open back, sound asleep.

"Maybe we should go a different way," I whispered to Margarete.

"Be calm," she said.

When the reading soldier saw us, he set down the book and jumped into the middle of the road, straightening his uniform as he did so. He held up one hand.

Margarete pulled on Blitz's reins and the wagon stopped.

"Where do you think you're going?" the soldier asked Margarete.

"I am taking my niece home," said Margarete in a firm voice.

"Papers." The soldier held out his hand.

I gulped.

Margarete handed over her own identification, and I reached into my skirt to get the one that said *Berta Pfaff.*

The soldier looked over both, then held mine up. I held my breath. "This is expired," he said.

"It is?" said Margarete, feigning surprise. She turned to me and said, "You'd better tell your father to get you a new one."

"We cannot let you pass with expired papers."

"Do you know who this girl's father is?" asked Margarete. "Can't you read *Pfaff*? Obersturmbannführer Pfaff is her father."

The soldier's face paled. He handed back our papers.

"What book is that?" she asked. "It doesn't look very official. I'm sure Berta's father would like to hear about the soldier who reads for pleasure while on duty."

The soldier ran his fingers through his hair. "Let's forget the whole thing," he said. "Have a safe journey."

He stepped off the roadway and waved us on. As we

passed, I smiled and waved. The man in the back of the truck hadn't woken up during the entire incident.

When we had driven a kilometer from the soldiers, I asked, "Are you really related to Obersturmbannführer Pfaff?"

Margarete smiled. "There is no such person."

"Then why did he let us pass?"

"That rank alone," said Margarete. "It is enough to terrify any soldier."

Soon the roads petered down to practically nothing— just bent grass in a field. We had been following the meandering river for some time, but now there was a thick line of trees up along the bank. Margarete pulled on Blitz's reins and the wagon stopped. We both stared at the trees. I had been waiting for this time, but now that it was in front of me, I was scared.

"This is where we should part company," said Margarete. She pointed up ahead. "Just keep following the river south and east. The woody areas are in patches; sometimes they're brush, then meadow, then swamp. There are houses too, now and then. Keep the river in sight and stay hidden. Avoid any well-used path."

I drew the identification papers out of my skirt and gave them back to Margarete. "Be well."

She gave me one last pat on the cheek and I jumped down to the ground, then shrugged on the heavy knapsack.

"Leave the girl's clothing on at least until you're hidden," she said. "Out here in the open, you'll draw less attention as a girl. A boy is safer in the woods."

I walked up to Blitz and buried my face in her mane. "Good-bye, old friend," I said.

I held my hand up in a final farewell as Margarete gave Blitz a light tap with the whip and they were off.

CHAPTER TEN
BIRCH

The knapsack pressed heavily against my back as I tried to walk quietly through the pine forest, but I felt like a thousand eyes were watching me. Each footstep made a loud crunch. How would I stay hidden if I couldn't stay quiet? And wouldn't stripping down and changing into men's clothing bring even more attention to myself? All the advice Margarete had given me seemed useless.

But if I was making this much noise, didn't that mean anyone else would also be making noise? The thought reassured me. I stood still and held my breath.

A low, insistent hum. But what made the sound? It was too late in the year for tree frogs or cicadas. The faint snap of a tiny twig. Was that a small animal scrambling away, or the sound of a person more used to hiding his movements in the forest than I was? I walked again, stopped suddenly, and listened for footsteps, but there were none. I kept on walking for another hour or so. The pine trees became interspersed with birch and then the woods became mostly birch. I stopped for a moment, breathing in the changed air. The scent of resin had given way to a faintly earthy smell of fallen autumn leaves.

I looked up into the sky and was awed by the stark beauty of the bare birch trees that surrounded me. All at once, it was as if I were standing in the middle of Bykivnia, the forest at the outskirts of Kyiv. How many times had I walked through the towering birch trees to visit my grandfather?

Each spring, David and I duck out of school and wander through the woods, picking wild berries. We eat our fill and bring some back to his father, who bakes them into tarts.

Grandfather has a special place in his heart for David, and whenever the two of us visit, he has some small treat waiting for each of us—a figure carved in wood, or oddly shaped pebbles. Once, he proudly presents each of us with fabric belts that he has woven himself, meticulously working in a zigzag pattern of brown and black felt. The one Dido himself has worn for years is similar, but with green added to the brown and black. "I would have made you ones like mine," he says, "but I can no longer get the green felt."

David and I love our handmade belts and wear them always.

The last time we look for berries together is the summer before Kyiv falls to the Nazis—during those final frenzied days when the Soviets are fleeing.

As we are walking through the familiar woods, David stops. "What caused that?" he asks, pointing to dark, glistening streaks on the path.

I bend down and touch it. Blood. "Maybe someone dragged a dead deer."

When we get to Dido's house half an hour later, we find him sitting at the worn kitchen table, a distracted look on his face. He seems somehow smaller, almost shrunken within himself.

He looks up at us with worried eyes. "Don't come back here."

"But why?" asks David. "We love visiting you."

"I hear ghosts," says Dido. "For two weeks now, their sighs have drifted through the woods, keeping me awake at night. This place is cursed."

He thrusts a bag of dried mushrooms into each of our hands and kisses us each on the cheek. "Go now."

On the walk home, we stand silently in the deepest part of the woods. David touches a finger to his lips. After a few minutes, I shake my head. I hear nothing. Only the wind sighing through the birch trees.

When we get back to the city, a scent of gasoline is in the air.

"This way," says David, grabbing my sleeve and pulling me into a back alley.

73

From the shadows we watch Soviet NKVD thugs strut-
ting down the street, their bayonets nudging a cluster of
handcuffed young men.

"That's Panas, isn't it?" David whispers, pointing at one
of the taller prisoners.

I nod, then recognize Myron, Dmitri, Volodymyr,
Myroslav, others—men who had been to our house before my
father was taken. All were at the university until the Soviets
kicked them out.

We watch the NKVD police march them out of the city
toward Bykivnia Forest.

"Come on," says David. "We've got to see what they're doing."

"Wait, David. Both our fathers have already been taken. If
you or I go missing, it would kill our mothers."

He sighs. "Sometimes you are so fearful."

"Sometimes you need to be more fearful."

How I wished now that David had been born with a
bit of my caution.

I tried to clear those images from my mind and focus
on the present. These woods I walked in held a different set of dangers than Bykivnia Forest in the summer
of 1941.

I followed along the river even as it meandered, because
it eventually would lead to the foothills of the mountains.

There might have been a shorter way, but why risk getting lost? I walked for a few hours, still wearing the girls' clothing, although I did slip the kerchief from my head and tie it around my neck. I ate half the bun. That made me think of David again, and the smell of his father's bakery. I could not get him out of my mind. It was almost as if he were walking beside me, urging me to be a little bit braver.

But like Bykivnia, this forest had its own ghosts.

It would have been smart to stop and change out of the girls' clothing, but I felt like I was being watched. Once it was dark, I could change.

I kept on walking, wanting to make as much headway as I could on my first day. It was irritating to have the skirt catch against my knees with every step. How did girls tolerate this? I could hardly wait until darkness fell and I could get out of these clothes.

I came upon a shallow stream around midmorning. I crouched down and scooped handfuls of the fresh, clear water and gulped it down. Sometime past midday, the forest gave way onto a huge burned area. Charcoal shards and sharp black spikes pointed to the sky. My boots squeaked and my nose itched from the smell of old smoke. I was suddenly filled with such grief it was like a blow to the head. My knees crumpled and I fell into the charcoal.

Memories from the summer of 1941—when the Nazis suddenly switched sides and attacked their former ally—flooded my mind. The Soviets had been running scared.

Stalin says that everything must burn in Kyiv. What won't burn must be destroyed. When the Nazis come, they must find nothing but ashes.

Throughout July and August, ashes fall like black snow, and dark clouds of smoke hang over Kyiv. NKVD police storm the government buildings, churches, and synagogues. They burn birth and death records, marriage certificates, journals, tax records. Ashes of history cling to my clothing. When I try to wipe them away, a powdery smear remains.

As August turns to September, we hear over the loudspeakers that the Nazis are at our gates. I am still cheering for our side, thinking that when the Nazis get here they'll be in for a beating.

But something strange happens.

The city leaders leave: the Communist mayor and administrators, the fire department, the police. With them, they take all the food that will fit into trucks and boxcars. They dismantle whole industries and take them too. And weapons. What they can't take, they douse with gasoline.

They leave behind the sick and the poor, and old people who are of no use to them anymore.

There are some who refuse to abandon Kyiv, but where have these brave souls got to? It's as if they are ghosts.

David and I go up the hill to our famous golden-domed Pecherska Lavra. Mama once said that it had been a Ukrainian Orthodox cathedral and monastery for a thousand years before the Soviets came. It has a network of tunnels underground. Some people say that the tunnels are hundreds of kilometers long, stretching all the way to Novgorod. When invaders came, Kyivans would escape through the tunnels. Now Pecherska Lavra is a Soviet museum. David and I like going there— running up and down the steps and walking around the ancient stone buildings. It's a great place to play soldiers.

But on this particular September day when we climb to the top level of Pecherska Lavra, he points toward my grandfather's place. Bykivnia Forest billows with black smoke. "Why would they burn down the woods?" he asks.

As I shade my eyes with one hand, I think of Dido's agitation the last time we saw him. My stomach churns. "Do you think Dido is okay?"

"Only one way to find out," says David.

We scramble down the steps and run through the cobblestone streets to the edge of town. When we get to the burning forest, NKVD soldiers block our way.

One of the soldiers steps forward—Misha. He lived on my

street and was a senior at Kyiv School #75 before the war. "It's not safe here," he says. "Go home."

"But my grandfather lives that way," I say, starting forward.

"I am sure he is fine," says Misha, not looking sure at all. He nudges me with his bayonet. "Go."

We leave, but I feel uneasy. Just days after that, the Nazis arrive. David and I watch in shock from the top of Pecherska Lavra as waves of Red Army soldiers set down their arms and surrender. Others flee. No one fights.

The Nazis remove the sandbags and the barbed wire that encircle Kyiv, then they march right in. They come with their clean uniforms, polished boots, and freshly scrubbed faces. They set up offices in the same buildings that the Soviets have just abandoned. At first they seem friendly. It looks like they are trying to create order.

Now that the NKVD no longer blocks the forest, I want to get through to see Dido again. As David and I head out toward the edge of the city, we meet up with others going the same way.

In the blackest part of the burned forest, we encounter a circle of people, their heads bent in grief. The sound of a woman's muffled keening sends chills down my spine. With David right behind me, I force my way to the inner part of the circle.

Clumps of freshly dug earth cling to stacks of corpses, most with ragged red holes in their necks or bayonet wounds in *their chests. They are almost all young men, and I recognize Myroslav—one of those we saw being marched out into the woods by those NKVD thugs.*

A woman who stands beside me reaches down and gently pulls a bit of paper loose from a woman's coat near the edge of the grave. As she unfolds it, I notice a spatter of blood and handwriting in a language I don't know.

"That's in Polish," says the woman. Her eyes fill with tears as she reads the words: "My name is Elzbieta Slawsky and I live on Krucza Street in Warsaw. Please give me a Catholic burial if you find me dead."

Poland is so far away. Have the Soviets brought her all this way just to kill her? My fists clench.

David grips my shoulder. He says, "Luka, I am so sorry." That's when I recognize a distinctive brown-black-green woven belt toward the middle of the mass grave. Even without seeing the face, I know it is Dido's corpse. I lunge to get to him, but David holds me back. "We must get out of this cursed place," he says.

CHAPTER ELEVEN
NOT KYIV

That scene from two years ago was all too sharp in my mind. The blackened shards of this German forest brought my grief to the surface. How could I go on? I bowed my head in despair.

A wet splat on the back of my neck.

I reached back to feel for blood. It was warm, but too gritty for blood. I held my hand in front of me—it was covered with a gray smear of bird poo.

For a moment I felt like shaking my fist at the bird, but I took a deep breath and gave thanks instead. I was not in Kyiv, and it was not 1941. It was two years later and I still had a chance to survive.

As I stood up and wiped the mess off my neck, fear replaced sadness. This forest was ever changing, and this clearing I stood in was too much in the open. I ran toward the trees, my lungs aching as they filled with sooty air.

Sweat streamed down me by the time I got out of the burned area. Now I was in a section with young fir trees no taller than my hips. Even a nearsighted Nazi would have no trouble finding me here!

I trekked down a hill through mud and brush to get close to the river and as far away from open view as I dared. The river changed as much as the forest, but here it was so wide that the other shore was not visible. The bank made for treacherous walking, and more than once I slipped, making my thigh throb. Once I stepped onto what looked like solid ground, only to have my boot sink down into mud. Just then a military barge stacked with wooden boxes passed by. I stood still, slowly sinking into the mud, and prayed that no one on the barge would notice me. When it had finally passed, I pulled myself out and crawled onto a big rock behind a bush, trembling with relief.

It had been a warm day for late November, but dusk brought a chill. I was wet with river mud and sweat, so the cool air made me shiver. My feet were sore and my leg hurt. Fir needles and leaves stuck to my mud-caked clothing, making me itchy.

I had walked beyond the young forest and was back in the midst of tall fir trees. Finally, a place that gave camouflage. I shrugged off the knapsack. It landed on the earth with a *thunk*. Next off was the filthy blouse and muddy skirt. I shook out the worst of the dried mud, and the remaining half of the bun tumbled out. I stowed the dirty clothing and bun in an outside pocket of the knapsack. As I stood with nothing on but underwear, filthy socks, and boots, I heard a loud snap. My heart nearly stopped.

I picked up the knapsack and quietly stepped behind a fir tree. My skin prickled in the cold as I held my breath and waited for whatever had made that noise to pass by. Nothing.

This was probably the worst possible time to remove my boots, but I was determined to get my trousers on. If I was captured, I preferred to die of something other than humiliation. Balancing on one foot, I removed the first boot and peeled off the wet sock, grimacing as a big hunk of skin from my heel came off with it. When I removed the second boot and sock, there was another broken blister, but this one wasn't as bad.

I pulled on my trousers and shirt, a warm jacket, and a dry pair of socks, my heart pounding until I got my boots back on and laced up. I leaned up against the tree and listened. The thing that had snapped the twig must have gone. The forest was eerily still.

I needed to find a secure place to rest for the night, but where? There weren't just soldiers to worry about. Wouldn't there be wild animals in the forest as well? But if I didn't rest, I'd be too worn out to get to the mountains. I shrugged the knapsack onto my back and walked through the thickest part of the woods—as far away from what seemed to be the walking path as I dared. I found a thicket of low bushes and worked my way in, the sharp branches scratching my face and snagging my hair. It wasn't the most comfortable place to sleep, but for the first time since entering the forest, I felt truly hidden.

Now that I was settled and secure, it would have made sense to find one of those boxed meals that Helmut and Margarete had given me, but I didn't want to use them up too quickly. I took out the last muddied half of a bun. That would do. I took one bite, then shoved the rest inside my shirt for later. As I chewed, my mind filled with memories of David again.

The Nazis are so smug when they take over Kyiv in September 1941. When they hear of the huge grave in the forest, they send a journalist. Soon after, the top layer of the grave is emptied and the bodies lined up. Kyivans are ordered to view the display. Each one of us goes, hoping that our own missing loved ones haven't made their grave in Bykivnia.

I already know that Dido is in that pit, and the thought of seeing his corpse lined up like a Nazi display makes me ill. But Mama and I need to go. What if Tato is there? Or David's father?

The four of us—me, Mama, David, and Mrs. Kagan—go together and wait in the sad lineup of keening women and children. The corpses are lined up in front of the forest, feet pointing toward Pecherska Lavra. One of the officers whispers to another that this top layer of bodies had been very fresh—executed over the summer—but that the pit seems limitless. He estimates there are one hundred thousand dead at least, and that the pit has been used for years. My mind can hardly grasp that figure. Is it even possible? Why would Stalin kill so many of his own people?

Bykivnia Forest is surely filled with ghosts. That's all I can think as we walk slowly from one body to the next, thankful each time that the victim isn't Tato. The air is heavy with sorrow and the only sounds are the gasps of recognition when a body is claimed. That, and the wind sighing through the birch trees.

The next day, an article appears in the Nazi newspaper about Bykivnia, but instead of blaming Stalin and the Soviet NKVD, the reporter says it was the Jews who have done the killings.

Mama crumples up the newspaper and throws it onto the floor. "They must think we're stupid," she mutters. "They blame everything on the Jews."

Mrs. Kagan looks at Mama and says, "It's Stalin's last cruel joke on us."

An owl hooted and Mrs. Kagan's image faded, but I couldn't get that scene from long ago out of my mind. I tried to turn, but the wiry bushes poked and prickled. I felt so imprisoned by the blackness of night and the cover of shrubs that I nearly panicked. Was this what it felt like to be buried within a mass grave? I tried to push that thought out of my mind. I was hidden—and almost safe. I was alive. I concentrated on that reality. I closed my eyes, but sleep would not come.

I took a deep breath and held it in my lungs for a moment, then let it out slowly. I did that a second time and a third. By the fourth breath, my heart had slowed down and I began to feel calmer. I opened my eyes. All around me was blackness deeper than coal. The sky was mostly obscured by branches, but if I concentrated, I could see the distant stars. That calmed me too, but still I could not sleep.

I wondered if Mama was looking up at the sky right now and seeing the same stars. Mama, Tato, Lida—the people I loved most—were scattered apart but still living, united under the same sky. "Please be safe," I prayed. Then I fell into a dreamless sleep.

CHAPTER TWELVE
FRIENDS

I dreamed I was wrapped tightly in sharp lengths of barbed wire. I opened my eyes: Not barbed wire, but prickling thorns and twigs enveloped me. I struggled, but they just dug even more into my arms and legs.

If I kept on struggling, the thorns would tear my skin apart. I took a deep breath. As I slowly exhaled, I thought of Lida. Even in the worst situations, she knew how to make things bearable, by singing a lullaby or giving a reassuring smile. I took another breath. I could get through this.

Lida . . . Again I regretted leaving her behind. But she knew that the hospital was an evil place. Had I not escaped, they would have killed me. If I could have taken her with me, I would have. Once the war was over, I would find her. I would not have the death of another dear friend on my conscience.

As I lay there fighting my memories, I listened to the occasional hooting of an owl or the snap of a twig. Behind the forest sounds was the ever-present rumble of bombs and planes and guns. Was I safe in my hiding place? Certainly safer than David had ever been, and more secure than Lida. But the forest chill crept into my bones and I felt utterly alone.

I dug into my shirt and broke off another piece of the bun. I held it to my face and breathed in the faint scent of cherry. I was thankful for all that Helmut and Margarete had given me. Their kindness was proof that everyone was capable of goodness.

I put it into my mouth, but it sat on my tongue like sawdust. I chewed and swallowed, determined not to waste a crumb. I thought of David and my heart ached with sorrow. I thought of Lida, a prisoner still, trying to survive on watery soup. How she would have savored just one small bite of a cherry bun.

My eyes slid shut . . .

Snow flutters down, blanketing my body with a damp chill. Snow on my feet—they are like giant balls of ice.

Lida sits before me, her badge that says OST *glowing in the darkness. She holds a thread and needle in one hand and a badge for me in another. I watch as she places it onto the front of my flannel shirt and begins to sew. But her needle plunges into my skin, drawing blood.*

I was jolted from my half dream by the odd sensation of pinpricks on my stomach. I reached inside my shirt . . . and got a handful of fur. Just then a squirrel, its teeth firmly sunk into the stale remains of the bun, darted out of my shirt. I grabbed the bun and the squirrel tugged, ripping away a big chunk. With a twitch of its tail, the squirrel raced off with its prize.

It was daylight. Had I really slept through the entire night in a prickly bush, unaware of everything, even a squirrel gnawing inside my shirt? I had been lucky. If I were to survive out in the open, I had to be more careful. It wouldn't do to depend only on luck.

Now that I had survived my first night, the forest seemed a friendlier place. I was hungry and thirsty, but didn't want to take the time to stop and root around in my knapsack, so I ate the last of the bun and kept on walking. The leaves were covered with dew and didn't crunch as I stepped on them. I found no more streams. I wanted to get down to the river and drink my fill of water, but the bank was high and steep and the water too fast. Instead, I chewed on dewy blades of grass and tried not to think about how dry my throat was.

I spied a few puffball mushrooms. Some varieties could be poisonous, but these weren't, and since dried puffballs were good at stanching blood, I gathered them up and put them in my knapsack.

I made good progress that day and oddly ran into no one. That night I dug down deep into a thicket and fell into an uneasy sleep.

Sometime in the middle of the night, I was jolted awake when the ground shook from a distant bomb. Memories of that time after Bykivnia rushed back to my mind.

A few days after the Nazis display the corpses in the woods, I wake up to the ground shaking. A piece of plaster falls from the ceiling and crashes down inches from my head. "What is happening?" I yelp, jumping out of bed.

"Come on," says David, slipping his feet into a pair of shoes.

When we get out to the street, a billow of smoke drifts beyond Pecherska Lavra. Many people mill about, startled awake like us.

"The Soviets planted a bomb in the arsenal before they left," says a man, breathlessly running down the street in his pajamas.

"It wasn't the Soviets," says an old woman with swollen

ankles sitting on the steps of a crumbling building. "It's probably the Jews again."

"How can you say such a thing?" I ask her.

"It talks about a similar incident right here," she says, pointing to an article in the Nazi paper. "And they've arrested some of the culprits."

The only Jews who are left in the city are the sick and elderly, women and children—not any different than the people left behind who aren't Jewish. Everyone who was important has been evacuated to safety. And we all know now that the young leaders of the city who were opposed to Stalin have been murdered at Bykivnia.

On September 24, we are ordered to register at the make-shift German government office in the old hotel on Svertlov Street. Thousands wait patiently in line as the new city clerks try their best to fill out the German forms.

When it is finally my turn, I notice that the clerks have three columns of names.

"Why do you have three lists?" I ask.

"Our Nazi leaders have more respect for your beliefs than the Soviets ever did," he says. "We're listing how many Jews, Russians, Ukrainians live here. That way the Nazis can reopen the right number of churches and synagogues."

I turn and leave, wondering about his comment. Does that

mean that they will turn Pecherska Lavra back into a monastery? An interesting idea.

I am a hundred meters away from the registration building when there is a loud, rumbling roar. Suddenly, I fly through the air, pieces of concrete raining on my back. I land on my hands in the cobblestone road, scraping my face, the wind knocked out of me. The upper floor of the toy store beside the registration building flies off in the explosion and lands on top of dozens of people waiting in line.

My face is wet with blood and the back of my shirt is in shreds. A frail man comes out from one of the houses and mops my face with his handkerchief. Just then a second explosion rocks the street. The registration building is engulfed in smoke and rubble.

"Another gift from Stalin," the man grumbles, folding up his bloodied handkerchief. "I guess we can expect another announcement that the Jews did it."

For the next two days, buildings explode every few minutes from bombs planted by the NKVD before they escaped. Soviet undercover agents throw Molotov cocktails, igniting buildings. Because the fire department has abandoned the city, a massive fire burns for a week and a huge cloud of ash hangs yet again over Kyiv.

We do all that we can to get the fires out, but the flames rage on. In retaliation, the Nazis shoot anyone who lives in a building beside one that burned—for not trying hard enough to put the fire out, they claim, though David says that they are just looking for excuses to kill us.

At dusk on the last Sunday in September, I stand on the roof of our communal flat, David beside me. All around, Kyiv burns.

"What is to become of us?" I ask.

David shrugs, then points to a soldier who is nailing a notice to a post down the street. "Let's go see what it says."

A small crowd gathers on the street in front of the sign, blocking our view. Someone at the front says, "They're ordering all the Jews to assemble near the cemetery on Monday at eight o'clock in the morning. They're to pack for travel."

As we walk back home, David says, "Where do you think they're going to take us?"

I think of Dido and all of the others in the graves, the explosions and fires, the clouds of black smoke hanging above. Deep down, I want David to stay, but I know that is selfish. If he and his mother can get to safety, they have to take the chance.

"Do you think any place could possibly be worse than here?" I ask him.

"They will probably send us to a work camp," says David.

Mama helps Mrs. Kagan sort through her meager possessions. Each traveler is allowed only a single suitcase.

"Photographs," says Mrs. Kagan, slowly turning the pages

in a worn family album and stopping somewhere around the middle. "These are more precious than food." She takes one out and turns it for us to see—a formal wedding shot of a hopeful-looking woman with serious eyes. Behind her stands Mr. Kagan—not looking much different than the last time I saw him, just younger.

She takes out a picture of David that makes me smile. He must have been about two, with curly hair like a girl.

"Of all the photographs you've got of me, you're keeping that one?" David asks, his face pink.

"You were a beautiful child," says his mother. "So innocent. Quit complaining."

Mama sorts through our shared pantry and divides out what little we have left—cracker bread, some apples, a few onions. "Take these," she says. "Who knows when you'll be fed."

The next morning, Mama and I walk with David and Mrs. Kagan to the train station. "I don't understand why the Soviets set off all those explosions," Mama says. "Surely they knew that the Nazis would blame the Jews."

"No matter what happens, we are always blamed," replies Mrs. Kagan bitterly.

It makes me angry to hear her say that, but it's true. The Soviets did this, and now the Nazis. Some things never change.

David wears his winter coat over his best suit, as well as three pairs of socks and two shirts. His mother also wears her heaviest coat, plus a sweater, three skirts, two scarves, and fur-lined boots that belonged to Mr. Kagan.

The street fills with people—some pushing wheelbarrows, others carrying awkward boxes on their backs. Two men carry a stretcher that holds an elderly rabbi. It isn't just Jews who come out. Friends and non-Jewish family walk alongside.

"I don't know why the Jews are the only ones to get evacu-ated," says a squat woman with a cane as she hobbles beside us. "Why are they so special? I'm going to see if they'll let me on the train as well—I don't know how much more I can take, breath-ing in this smoke."

We walk down Melnikov Street with crowds of other people, watching the soldiers lining the road. Some hold clubs, others rifles. A few hold back fierce-looking dogs. "We're doing as they asked," says David. "I don't see why they have to be out in such force."

I do a double take when I see, close to the end of the row of soldiers, a face that is etched in my mind. Sasha, the Soviet NKVD who took Tato away—now in a Nazi uniform. Beside him stands Misha, yet another former NKVD thug. I tug on Mama's sleeve and motion with my eyes.

She nods. "Bullies are all the same, no matter what uniform they wear," she says. "I recognize a few former Soviets who rel-ished tormenting us then, and now they just do it in another uniform."

Suddenly a block of German soldiers stands in our way. "Papers," says one, reaching out his free hand. The other restrains a German shepherd. Behind the soldiers, a line of trucks idles, stacked high with suitcases, boxes, and bags.

All four of us hold out our identification papers. "You two," he says to David and Mrs. Kagan. "Put your luggage on one of the trucks, then go through."

He turns to me and Mama. "No farther. Go home now."

I hold my hand out to David and give it a firm shake. "Good luck," I say.

David's eyes look sad, but he pastes a brave smile onto his face. "Don't forget me, Luka," he replies. Then he and his mother walk through the cordon of soldiers.

I never saw him again.

Two days later, we found out that there had been no train. The Nazis had murdered the Jews of Kyiv. Their bullet-riddled bodies now filled the ravine of Babyn Yar.

CHAPTER THIRTEEN
FIGHTING BACK

I could still almost hear David's voice saying, "Don't forget me, Luka."

An overwhelming weariness washed over me.

I vowed to survive this horrible war so I could tell others about what the Nazis had done and how David had been killed. David would have loved Lida. Had he lived, they could have been the greatest of friends.

I untangled myself from the branches and started back on my journey.

The woods seemed oddly empty. Surely I wasn't the only one in them. I walked until the midday sun broke through the branches overhead and didn't see a single soul. Once, a deer darted by in the distance, and another time I nearly stepped on a snake, but the birds were oddly silent and I saw no trace of other humans.

I walked as close to the edge of the river as I dared,

waiting for a spot where I would be able to climb down and get a drink, but long stretches of the bank were too soft and crumbly for climbing. In places, the bank plunged right down to deep churning water. Finally, I came upon a stretch that overlooked a pebbled beach and a patch of river that rippled but didn't churn. Perhaps it was shallower.

Using the roots of trees as a ladder, I climbed down to water level. I stayed hidden behind some bushes and watched for a few minutes to make sure no one else was around. I stepped over mucky stones until I reached a dry, flat rock, then shrugged the knapsack off my shoulders and sat down. It was so silent and still, and watching the river ripple over smooth rocks had a soothing effect. I could almost forget that I was a fugitive in the midst of a war.

I set my knapsack on the rock and picked my way from one rock to another until the river looked knee-deep. I knew I was taking a risk, but there wasn't a single boat in sight and the opposite bank was deserted.

I knelt down and took huge gulps of water, then splashed my face and hair. It felt so good to finally not be thirsty. I used the stepping-stones to get back to the flat rock and stretched out. It was chilly, but I was relieved to be out of the woods. My stomach grumbled. This was as good a time as any to open up one of those American army rations and see what they contained. I reached for my knapsack.

It was open.

Had I left it that way? I couldn't remember. I took everything out of it, placing the extra clothing Margarete had packed over to one side. There was also a first-aid kit. Thank you, Margarete and Helmut! A stiff piece of fabric was folded tightly and tucked along the back of the knapsack. I pulled it out and unfolded it—a huge lightweight rain poncho with a camouflage pattern—very useful. But then I counted and stacked the ration boxes and there were only nine. I was sure there were supposed to be ten.

Perhaps one had dropped out of the knapsack? Or maybe there were only nine to begin with. In any case, I'd had my fill of water and that would have to do for now. I packed everything back up and slipped on the knapsack. I was halfway up the riverbank when the scent of roasting meat drifted toward me. My stomach growled with hunger.

There *were* other people around. Had one of them stolen a ration box from my knapsack? But why would they steal just one and leave everything else? It didn't add up. Whatever the truth was, I was suddenly aware of how exposed my location was.

I quietly climbed back up part of the bank until I could

just peek over the edge. At first I saw nothing, but the aroma of smoke and meat directed me to a clearing a stone's throw away. Leaning against a thick fir tree was a German soldier, cleaning a rifle. At his feet was a second rifle. A smoky fire billowed a few meters away and another soldier squatted on the ground in front of it, holding a sausage on a stick over the flames.

Here I was, trying hard to hide, and these two soldiers were so oblivious to the dangers of the forest that they were out in the open, roasting meat. What could it possibly mean? Did they feel immune to danger because they had guns? Or maybe they were part of a bigger group combing the woods for escapees like me?

The water that I had gulped down now felt like it was coming up. I had to get away. I slid down so they wouldn't be able to see the top of my head. I'd have to wait here until they finished their meal and left, but what if there *were* others? I would surely be caught.

Just then a twig snapped. Suddenly a girl about my age appeared out of the brush near the embankment. Her face was smudged with soot and on her feet were old-fashioned *postoly*—soft handmade leather slippers—over thick wool leggings. Her ragged clothing blended in with the muddy bank. She held two halves of a broken twig up for me to see—she'd snapped it on purpose to get my attention. She put one finger to her lips for silence, but there was a smile in her eyes.

Keeping her gaze locked onto mine, she slowly flipped open a satchel that she wore across one shoulder and drew out my missing ration box. She grinned at my look of outrage, then stepped closer.

She leaned against me as if we were friends, then quietly opened the ration box and took out two biscuits. She pressed one into my palm and nibbled on the corner of a second one.

Wasn't she afraid that the soldiers above us could hear her eating the biscuits? But if she was going to eat one, I would too. I could be as brave as her.

I took a small bite and swallowed, trying to sort out just what was happening. Did the girl have something to do with the soldiers? Why would she steal from me, only to then share with me?

The voices of the soldiers drifted down to us.

"I don't know how we got so far off track from the rest of them," said one voice.

"Never mind," said the other. "They've likely headed back to the base."

"Shouldn't we keep looking for runaways?"

"There's no one here," the second man muttered. "We've been up and down this entire section."

I could hear stomping and twigs snapping—probably them putting out the fire—then footsteps all too close. "It's so quiet here," said the one soldier who had to be standing right above me. I plastered myself against the bank and held my breath.

"Come, Willy, let's go."

The voices and footsteps drifted away, but I stayed frozen in place, leaning against the embankment. The girl stayed still as well. After a few minutes she quietly reached into the box and drew out a second biscuit for each of us.

As I chewed, she said in a voice that was low like the wind, "They're gone." The language she used sounded like heavily accented Ukrainian. Then she turned to me. "Now, who are you?"

I glared at her. "None of your business."

"Where did you come from?" she asked.

I didn't like her questions, and her familiarity confused me. For all I knew, she was working with the Nazis. She could turn me in at any moment if she knew I had escaped from a slave-labor camp.

When I didn't answer right away, she said, "From your accent, I'd guess Kyiv, but you didn't arrive in these woods directly from there, did you? What's your story?"

"What's *yours*?" I shot back. "Are you working with those soldiers?"

"*With* them? I just saved your life."

"All you've done is steal my food."

"Not so loud," she whispered. "Let's find a better place to talk." She clambered up the roots and hoisted herself onto the forest floor, then waited while I did the same. "This way."

She climbed up into the very same fir tree that just moments before the soldier had leaned against. The campfire still smoldered in front of it. I stood there for a moment, watching as she scrambled up the tree, then disappeared through the boughs. Finally her head poked out. "Aren't you coming?" she asked.

I followed.

She moved with such ease that I knew it was second nature for her, and I tried to keep up, but she was incredibly swift. Finally she sat down in the crook of a branch and patted the spot beside her. I sat too, taking deep, slow breaths. I didn't want her to realize how winded I was.

She pointed down through a break in the branches. "See that?"

I looked where she pointed but didn't see anything remarkable.

"The bends in the leaves show the soldiers' boot prints."

Once she pointed them out, I could see them clearly.

"*You* left your giant clumping boot prints all over the forest," she said. "I've been following you all morning."

"But why?"

She rolled her eyes. "So you'd live. I walked behind you and covered your tracks. Those soldiers would have found you otherwise."

No wonder there had been no birds chirping. They had noticed all the activity, but I hadn't. And here I thought I'd been honing my survival skills. How humiliating to owe my life to a girl—and one who was likely younger than me, about ten or so. "Why would you want to save my life?" I asked her.

"I'm guessing you're an escaped slave laborer, like me. You don't seem to have the survival skills of a spy. But maybe you're only pretending." She held out her hand. "My name is Martina Chalupa, and I'm Czech."

I shook her hand. Her fingers gripped mine with surprising strength. "Were you in a labor camp?" I asked.

She shook her head. "A farm."

"Are there others like you out here?"

She looked at me with troubled eyes. "Many escape, but few survive. This whole area is swarming with Nazi bandit hunters. They'll kill you on sight."

"So what do I do now?"

"Do you want to travel with me?" asked Martina.

"It depends," I said. "Where are you going?"

Martina sighed. "I don't really know. I've just been trying to stay alive and safe."

"I want to get to the mountains," I told her. "And as far away from the war as I can."

"I'd like to get away from the war too," she said.

"Let's travel together, then," I said. "We can look out for each other."

Martina smiled.

"So what do we do now?" I asked.

"Nothing."

"We can't just stay here."

"Rule one of surviving in the woods: move by night, hide by day." She pointed to my boots. "Do you have to wear those?"

Her question surprised me. "These are valuable."

"You can't feel what you're stepping on."

"I was barefoot when I escaped," I said. "I stepped on some glass when I was running, and cut my heel. It's barely healed even now. I need these boots."

She looked at me skeptically. "I'll try to teach you how to walk quietly, then—even with boots." She reached into her pouch and brought out a dented metal flask.

"Hold these," she said, unscrewing the top and thrusting the cap and flask toward me. Next she opened up the ration box she'd stolen from me and drew out a small foil packet. "You don't even know what this is, do you?"

She ripped the packet open with her teeth and sprinkled the contents into her flask, screwed the cap back on, and shook it. She poured some into the cap and passed it to me. I took a sip—sweet and fruity. "Tastes good."

Martina sipped the rest of the capful and smiled. "I know. There are several kinds of ration boxes and they all contain something good. One has something like a beef broth. Another has coffee. Another has pure sugar." She screwed the top back on and placed the flask back into her pouch.

I thought of the nine other boxes in my knapsack and realized just how generous Helmut and Margarete had been. I was about to speak, but Martina's attention was drawn to something down below. She held a finger to her lips.

I followed her gaze. Three German troopers shuffled along, their heavy boots snapping twigs and rustling leaves. The tallest stopped directly underneath us, planting his feet at the edge of the fire.

"Look at that," he said to the other two, pointing at the wisps of smoke. "Willy and Johann must have been here. Sloppy idiots." He nudged the smoking ground with the tip of his boot, and the smoldering sticks loosened. "They could start a forest fire."

"I'll fix that," said the smallest of the three. He unzipped his pants and aimed a steady stream of urine on the sticks until there was no more smoke; then the three walked on.

It took my heart a while to stop pounding from another close call. If Martina hadn't decided to help me, I might have been long dead by now.

The boughs were narrow and itchy, and my hands were sticky with sap from climbing up, but we didn't want to risk finding someplace more comfortable, so we napped in fits and starts until night, then climbed down the tree and continued our journey.

It took some practice to move in the dark, and I couldn't walk as quietly as Martina, but she showed me how to place my entire boot down on the ground with slow, even pressure, to avoid making twigs snap. And I stepped onto the spots where she had already been, to minimize any signs of disturbance. She also showed me how to cover my tracks in open areas by sweeping over my footsteps with a branch. With Martina leading the way, we traveled quite far that first night.

At dawn she showed me how to go into the deepest part of a tangle of bushes and make a sleeping hole. We lined the bottom with fir branches, put the poncho on top of us like a blanket, then camouflaged it with more branches. We were snug and warm and completely hidden. I couldn't remember feeling this safe since before the war.

Martina opened up her leather satchel, pulled out the ration box again, and took out a small round tin. "These usually contain either meat or cheese," she said. She turned the tin upside down and pulled off a small metal key from the bottom. "You open it with this."

I watched as she inserted a little metal tab from the side of the tin into the key slot, then twisted. There was a faint popping sound and a farty smell. Martina wrinkled her nose. "Cheese," she said. "There'll be a spoon in here somewhere." She dug through to the bottom of the box, held up a tiny wooden paddle, and took out a package of crackers and spread on some cheese, then gave it to me.

The fact that it looked and smelled disgusting didn't stop me from putting the entire thing in my mouth and chewing. "Not bad," I mumbled.

"Anything is good when you're starving," said Martina, shoving a cheese-covered cracker into her own mouth.

"What else is in that box?" I reached in and pulled out another small package: cigarettes and matches. Too bad it wasn't something more to eat.

"There will be sweet biscuits, crackers, powdered drinks, candy, and either canned meat or cheese in each one," said Martina. "Some have cigarettes, others have a candy bar."

After we finished our supper, we settled down to sleep, but I was wide awake. Martina and I had traveled a whole night together and it was nearly dawn, yet we still barely knew each other.

"Once we get to the mountains, what are you going to do?" she asked.

"Stay as far away from the fighting as I can," I told her. "As soon as the war is over, I want to get back to Kyiv and find my father." I told her about how he had been taken to Siberia.

"Maybe it's safer in Siberia than in the war zone," she said.

"That's what I'm hoping," I told her. "He'll go back to Kyiv, I'm sure of that. I also have a friend at the slave camp I escaped from—Lida. Her parents were killed and her sister is lost and I'm like her big brother. After the war, I need to go back and find her. My mother was taken to Germany as an Eastern worker too, so if she can't make her way back to Kyiv, I'll have to find her as well."

Martina shared bits of what she had lived through. Her father had been in the Czech Underground—one of the people responsible for the assassination of General Heydrich, the officer in charge of Nazi-occupied

Czechoslovakia. This had been a huge success for the Underground, and people had cheered when they heard of it. For the people involved, it must have felt so good to be able to fight back for a change. But the Nazis had been furious, and applied what they called "collective responsibility" for the assassination. They had burned down Lidice, Martina's village. They executed the men, women, and most of the children. Those who weren't killed outright were sent to death camps.

"I have always been good at hiding," Martina went on. "I managed to get to my grandmother's village and I was safe for a few weeks, but then the Nazis came, looking for escaped laborers. Grandmother begged for them to take her instead of me, but they just laughed. They took us both."

"Where is your grandmother now?" I asked.

Martina looked down at her hands. "She died in the boxcar on our way to Germany."

"I am so sorry," I said. "How long have you been living in the woods?"

"Since the early summer," she said. "I've staked out a territory of a few kilometers and know it like my own hand. A lot of fugitives come through this way, so I help as many as I can." She grinned. "I disrupt as many German soldiers as possible."

Now that I had met Martina, I wanted to stay with her. From the conversation I had overheard between Officer Schmidt and his parents, I knew that the Soviets were closing in on the Reich. And from the map in that old atlas, I figured that this Polish-Czech borderland would be in the middle of battles between the Soviets and the Nazis. "Why don't you come away with me?" I asked. "We can get to the mountains together—far away from the fighting."

Martina was silent for a bit, then replied. "I'd like that."

"If we split one ration box between us each day," I said, "we could make them last nine days."

"We can stretch them out further by eating roots and grasses," she said.

We had three days of good luck—no rain, traveling twenty or more kilometers each night, and bedding down during the day, unnoticed in shallow holes, covered in layers of fir boughs. More than once, Martina spotted bandit hunters soon enough for us to hide. "We should make it to the mountains in about a week at this rate," I said.

But as we got farther away from the Reich, the woods began to fill with people who seemed to be like us— runaways—or locals poorly outfitted for travel and with fear in their eyes.

One day as we hid on the high limb of a tree, a girl who reminded me of Lida limped below us on bare, bloodied feet. I jabbed my elbow into Martina's ribs to get her attention, then pointed. "We've got to help her," I whispered.

Martina put a finger to her lips. She nodded toward a spot a few meters away. A German bandit hunter, rifle poised, was aiming at the girl's back.

He fired. The girl fell hard onto the leaves. A patch of red formed on her back.

My first instinct was to get down from the tree, to save her, but I knew it was already too late. And the bandit hunter was still standing there. He walked up to the girl's body and nudged it with the tip of his boot. Once he was sure she was dead, he walked away, leaving her where she was—perhaps as a warning to others.

At nightfall we climbed down from the tree. The girl still lay there, the ground around her now sticky with blood. She reminded me so much of Lida.

"We cannot just leave her here," I said.

"I agree," said Martina. "But we must be fast."

I took the skirt from Margarete out of my knapsack and wrapped it around the girl. Martina held my knapsack while I gathered the corpse into my arms. I felt so utterly sad for this poor girl who had barely lived, and now was dead. I thought of the people who loved her when she was alive, and who wouldn't even know how or where she had died. And of course it made me wonder about Lida. What was happening to her? Was she safe? Was she still in the camp, or had she escaped by now? I could only hope.

"This way," said Martina, walking away from the pathway and into the deepest part of the brush. Small twigs scratched at my face, and the ground was so uneven I was afraid of falling, but I held on to the girl and kept walking.

"Place her there," said Martina, pointing to a clearing under a low tree. I set her down, then Martina and I covered her with dry leaves and rocks. It wasn't a proper burial, but it was all that we could do. It was better than leaving her on the pathway for all to see.

CHAPTER FOURTEEN
NOT SEEING

We had traveled for ten days or more. The closer we got to the mountains, the colder it became. I had my jacket and the poncho, and Martina and I traded them back and forth, but one of us was always cold. The poncho was good for rain, but it was just a thin layer of fabric. Martina's handmade shoes had been useful for creeping soundlessly through the forest in the fall, but now that it was so cold out, she risked frostbite or being injured on icy rocks.

We ran out of ration boxes just as the mountains loomed large and the temperatures plunged.

After a night of walking through bitter wind and ice pellets, the morning was no better. We were plunged into a blizzard. "If we fall asleep in this," I said, "we'll freeze to death."

Martina's lips were blue and her face was gaunt with

hunger, but she smiled. "The good thing about this snow-storm is that it's hard to see through."

"A *good* thing?"

"Maybe the bandit hunters will stay inside. Maybe we can get to a village and beg for supplies."

"It's worth a try," I said. "There's not much else we can do anyway."

The snow was heavy enough to cover our footprints, but when we got to the edge of the forest, Martina sud-denly pulled me behind a tree.

A single soldier in white camouflage walked past, a mere meter in front of us. I held my breath and willed myself to be absolutely still.

He kept on walking.

Martina followed behind him, and I followed her. Each of us stepped carefully into the footprints that he had already made.

The man approached a military truck that was idling on the roadway. We hid behind a tree and listened.

"This area is clear," he said to the soldier at the steer-ing wheel.

"Get in, then," said the driver.

We watched as they drove down the road. I was hop-ing they would keep going, but I heard the truck idle once again and the *smack* of doors opening and closing. They hadn't gone far at all. They were methodically checking the entire area.

Martina grabbed on to my hand and pulled me out from behind the tree. She darted across the road, not paying any attention at all to the footsteps she was making. I felt like shouting at her, telling her to stop, but the soldiers would hear me. I had no choice. I had to follow her.

When we got across the road, I could barely see a thing through the blinding white of the storm, except the silhouette of a small building up ahead. Once we got to it, I saw that it was a peasant cottage similar to the one my grandfather had lived in. The wooden door hung uselessly on broken hinges, and drifts of snow had formed on the threshold.

Martina paused at the doorway for just a moment, then stepped over the snowdrift and inside. I followed.

A wooden kitchen table was overturned. Shards of pottery lay scattered over the floor. Something that looked like it had been meat stew was frozen in solid splats around an upended copper pot by the hearth.

I opened up a wooden storage box. Clothing for a young child, a Bible, hand-carved wooden toys. "There's nothing here for us," I said.

Martina took a wooden ladle from the hearth for herself and handed me a set of tongs.

I watched her tap various places on the walls and floor, and then I understood. She was listening for a hollow sound.

I followed her lead, tapping and listening. Suddenly she got down on her knees and ran her fingers along the edge of a row of tiles. Her fingers slipped into an opening and she tried to pull, but it wouldn't give. I got down beside her and together we dug our fingers under the narrow lip and tugged. All at once, a trapdoor yawned open.

An injured woman holding a sleeping boy stared up at us with pleading eyes. "Please don't hurt us."

The woman refused to come up, so we went down, closing the door behind us. The hiding place was lit with a couple of candles and it was much warmer than the woods, but a cold draft of air blew in from somewhere.

In the dim interior stood a bucket of water and an opened sack of dried bread, and wooden shelves holding a few jars. Another wall was covered with cloth. From the rafters hung bundles of onions, garlic, beets. The woman had a bruise on her cheek and blood crusted on her brow.

"Is the child sick?" I asked her.

"No," she said. "I gave him a paste made from poppy pods to keep him quiet. I was afraid the soldiers would hear him."

I rooted around in my knapsack and brought out the first-aid kit. "Can I take a look at your scalp?"

116

She lowered her head and held the candle close to it. There was a ragged gash just above her eye, but it was no longer bleeding. I gently cleaned the dried blood with a damp rag, being careful not to disturb the scab that had formed on the wound itself. "The soldiers did this?" I asked.

"They took my husband and older son," she said. "They left me for dead."

"And the boy?"

"He was down here, sleeping. They didn't know about him."

"You can't be giving him poppy pods every day. He'll die."

She pushed away my hand that held the bloodied rag and glared at me. "Do you think I don't know that? But what else can I do? I can't let them find us."

I dabbed some iodine gently across the scab. "You're right," I said. "They would hear the child. They've gone for now, but they could be back."

She shrugged. "I don't know what the answer is."

The woman looked at me more closely, then at Martina. I'm sure we looked awful—dirty and thin and too young to be of any help. But from her expression, I could see that she was beginning to relax. "What do you want?"

"Can you help us get some warm clothing, maybe some food?" asked Martina. "We want to get away from here."

"Eat this now," the woman said, giving each of us a piece of dried bread from her bag. "Find a place on the floor to sleep. I'll see what else I can do for you."

I took the poncho out of the knapsack and spread it on the floor. It was such a luxury to be indoors that Martina and I were asleep within minutes.

When I opened my eyes some hours later, the first thing I saw was a gray woolen coat draped over Martina as she slept. I sat up.

"That is all I could get," said the woman. "No boots— I'm sorry. But here's some food."

She set a small burlap bag beside me on the floor. I opened it—dried salted fish and a chunk of smoked pork fat. Good traveling food. I knew better than to ask where she got these things. No need to make her feel bad about taking things from a nearby house where the people were already dead.

"Thank you," I said.

Martina sat up, rubbing sleep out of her eyes. She noticed the coat draped over her. "Is this for me?" she asked. The woman nodded.

"We'll be on our way," I said. "You have been most generous."

"The snowstorm is over," said the woman. "And it's

118

nighttime. But you can't leave the way you came—your footsteps would show in the new snow. Come this way."

She drew back the cloth that covered one wall to reveal a low tunnel dug into the earth. "If you go that way," she said, pointing to the left, "it will take you under the path and into the woods."

All at once, I understood. Not all of the villagers had been killed or had escaped to the woods. Some were still here, hidden.

Martina got into her new coat and I put the food in my knapsack. "Stay safe," I said to the woman. "And thank you for helping us." She nodded, then dropped the cloth back down.

We crawled the length of the tunnel in pitch-darkness, our hands reaching up to the dirt walls to keep our balance. I thought about Pecherska Lavra in Kyiv and all the tunnels under it. How many connected tunnels were hidden under this small village and other villages too? I hoped the Nazis would never find them.

CHAPTER FIFTEEN
MUSHROOMS

Over the next week or so, snow alternated with winter rain, and when we arrived at the foothills of the mountains, the terrain gradually became more dangerous. We no longer had a big river to follow, as it had split up into creeks and marshes and little lakes. The mountains loomed large before us.

We needed to make the dried fish and smoked pork fat last as long as possible, because who knew how we would find food once we were up in the mountains and winter had truly set in. We kept our eyes open for edible greens— a rare find. We would see late-fall mushrooms, but I knew from Tato that most of them had to be cooked to draw out the poison, and cooking was out of the question if we wanted to stay hidden.

One moonlit night, Martina stopped suddenly. "Look," she said, crouching by a fallen tree. "Aren't these oyster mushrooms?"

I knelt beside her and took one in my hand. This mushroom had a pale, smooth cap and curled-down edges like an oyster mushroom should. I flipped it over. The gills looked firm. "They are," I said.

"Sometimes we ate these raw," said Martina.

"Mama always cooked them," I said. "But just slightly."

We gathered up a dozen or so and wrapped them in a cloth, then Martina put them into her satchel and we continued on our way.

As dawn broke, we dug a hole and lined it with fir boughs as usual. Once we were nested in and thoroughly hidden, Martina brought out two mushrooms and our flask of water. I got out a piece of dried fish for each of us.

The mushroom was sweet and fresh and tasted so good along with the fish. I reached into Martina's satchel and took out two more, then handed her one.

"Not right now," she said, putting it back. She turned on her side and within minutes was fast asleep.

I ate my second mushroom, savoring the taste and the fact that it filled my stomach. I closed my eyes and was asleep before I knew it.

Some hours later, I woke up with my stomach roiling in pain. It must have been that second mushroom. I had to relieve myself or I would burst. I pushed up one fir branch and looked outside. Bright sunlight hit my eyes, but there was no one around. It was probably midday—the worst time to be out—but I had no choice. If I stayed where I was, I would foul all our gear. If I was lucky, I could get out, relieve myself, and get back into our hiding place without Martina waking up. She would be furious if she caught me out in the middle of the day.

I slipped out of our hideaway and crept to a wooded gully a few meters away. I had just finished my business and was zipping up my trousers when the ground shook. I scrambled behind a thick tree and held my breath. The ground trembled again.

Moments later a woman passed, barefoot and wild-eyed, carrying a coat and boots. What had made the earth shake? What had she run from? I had to find out if we were in immediate danger before I went back to our hideout.

I darted from one tree to the next, keeping hidden all the way. Finally, I came to an opening in the woods where I could see down to a scattering of cottages along a country road. Along the near side of the road rolled a long line of dull gray Soviet tanks, their guns aimed toward the houses. It seemed odd that the Soviets would aim tanks at remote cottages.

I was trying to puzzle it out when, all at once, a row of green German tanks crested the hill behind the houses.

As if on cue, they lowered their guns, aimed at the Soviet tanks, and fired with a deafening roar. The Soviet tanks fired back and the ground shook again. The thatched roof of one cottage flew off, flaming. The door burst open and a man ran out, a toddler in his arms. He headed toward me.

I realized what I was witnessing: The war zone. The Front. It was right here.

I ran back to our hiding place and threw back the boughs. Martina had bolted up to a sitting position, her eyes wild. Just then the ground shook again.

"We have to get out of here!" I shouted. "Tanks! Down that way!" I grabbed my knapsack, Martina slung on her satchel, and we ran toward the mountains—and, we hoped, away from the Front.

I had lost track of the dates, but by the time we got to the mountains, it had to be mid-December. The days were more often snowy than wet. Sheer ice, rocky hills, and deep crevasses made traveling so difficult. The entire mountainside was crisscrossed with paths, some surely made by escaped slave laborers who were lost, and others made by people from the area who knew where they were going. But how could we tell which was which? As we hid in the trees or dug our way into holes with branches to cover us, we prayed for luck.

Beyond the canopy of firs, we could hear airplanes. More than once, we ducked for cover as a fighter plane strafed the treetops, shooting blindly as it barreled overhead.

We were increasingly hungry as our food ran out, as well as cold and frightened. I began to doubt the wisdom of trying to escape to the mountains. Maybe we should have stayed in that village with the woman and her son. But staying there would have felt like giving up. Even though the war seemed to be following in our footsteps, I had to get back to Kyiv to find my father.

We were so close to the battle areas that we'd see escaped Red Army soldiers, with disintegrating boots and frostbitten cheeks, limping past us as we hid. From time to time we would also see German soldiers who had given up, and escapees from the camps. Young people wearing homespun clothing would pass by too. It was as if the entire world had decided to escape to the mountains.

Once, in the blackest part of night, our way was completely blocked by a raging creek. We walked along it, hoping to find a spot without treacherous rocks jutting upward. We were both shivering by the time we found a spot that looked narrow enough to cross.

I grabbed a long branch from the ground and plunged

it into the water to see how deep it was. Close to the bank, it was just a few centimeters, but it dropped off steeply after that.

"How can we cross?" I asked Martina. "We'll be soaked, and once we're soaked, we'll freeze."

"Keep those precious boots of yours dry," said Martina. "We've got to go in barefoot."

She was right. I took off my boots and socks and stuck them in my knapsack. I rolled my pants up while Martina took off her ragged *postoly*. Holding each other's hands for balance and courage, we stepped into the creek together.

The shock of cold pierced through to my bones. At the halfway point, my foot plunged down a hole and I smacked hard into the icy water. My knapsack filled up and its weight pulled me down. I flailed in panic, until all at once both my feet touched ground. I tried to stand, but the current was too strong, and the knapsack pulled me down again.

Then the weight of it disappeared.

"I've got the knapsack," said Martina.

I managed to get my balance. Martina struggled to hold the knapsack as the current fought her for it. I reached out and grabbed one strap. Together we heaved it onto a jagged stone on the other side of the creek and it stayed there.

We groped our way toward that bank, slipping

dangerously with each step. I fell several times, as did Martina, but finally I pushed her onto the shore. I could barely claw my own way out of the water.

We pulled our sopping shoes back on and stumbled to our feet. Martina gripped me by the elbow and we trudged forward, exhausted, but happy to be across the river.

As we stumbled into the woods, a firm voice said, "Stop."

CHAPTER SIXTEEN
VERA AND ABRAHAM

The soldier's military overcoat was of an unfamiliar design. I watched, shocked, as he unbuttoned it and wrapped it around Martina, completely enveloping her. A second soldier looked like the perfect Nazi, with his ice-blue eyes and light brown hair, but he took his coat off and wrapped me in it.

What kind of Nazi would do that for a person like me? The heat from his coat felt uncommonly hot.

"Sorry about this," he said, taking a piece of cloth from his pocket and blindfolding me with it. Then I felt one strong arm gripping underneath my knees and the other under my back. He clutched me close to his chest and walked through the woods on sure feet.

I blacked out.

• • •

In my half-awake state, I tried to get my bearings. I was tucked into a narrow bed. Water trickled somewhere close by. The air smelled stale and moist, and my head throbbed. I opened one eye. I was in a dim room with walls of whitewashed wooden planks, cramped with three cots in addition to mine. The only light came from narrow slits in the ceiling high above. The rest of the ceiling was branches.

Across from me lay Martina. A train track of fresh stitches, glistening with blood, ran across her cheek. Her feet, which poked out from under a rough blanket, were wrapped in gauze.

"Martina," I whispered, sitting up woozily. "Wake up." Her eyelids fluttered but didn't open.

The third cot was empty, but in the fourth, below Martina's feet, lay a sleeping Wehrmacht soldier with white-blond hair who looked to be in his teens. One arm was in a cast and his face was much cleaner than his muddy uniform. A thick square of gauze covered much of his neck. Blood seeped through the gauze, slowly making a wet circle.

Where were we? A place for *Germans* to recuperate, obviously. What would they do to us when they realized we were runaway slave laborers?

Just then a tired-looking woman stepped through the doorway. Her outfit was a combination of Soviet and

German military uniforms, but the *postoly* on her feet were peasant wear.

She knelt by the German's cot and lifted the gauze at his neck, mumbling something under her breath in Ukrainian.

I felt entirely confused. If I knew for certain which side this woman was working for, I could play along—get myself and Martina out somehow—but nothing added up.

She left the room, but moments later came back with a tray of medical instruments. I watched as she removed the old dressing from the soldier's neck. A long wound had been stitched, but the middle part was still bleeding. She washed off the blood with antiseptic and dressed it again with a fresh bandage.

She cleaned the tray and set it on my cot, then looked at my forehead and said in Ukrainian, "It seems that your wound needs dressing as well."

My hand shot up to my forehead. On my left temple— just where it throbbed the worst—was a thick wad of gauze.

"I am sorry to say that we had to shave off some of your wonderfully wild hair in order to close the gash."

I managed to ask, "Who are you?"

"You can call me Vera," she said. "Field doctor for the Red Cross."

"Where are we?"

"An underground hospital," she said.

I looked up at the slits in the ceiling and suddenly realized why they gave so little light. It wasn't just the branches covering them—the slits themselves were as narrow as my little finger. All at once I felt like I was being smothered.

Vera put her hand on my forearm. "Relax," she said. "It's normal to feel closed in at first."

I lay back down on the cot and stared at the slits of light, trying to breathe slowly, trying not to think about the fact that I was so deep under the ground.

"You're lucky to be alive," said Vera as she gently pulled off the old bandage on my brow. "Stefan and Danylo found you just a hundred meters from the battle zone. Even if you and your friend had managed to survive your plunge in the creek, you would surely have been shot."

Just then a rhythmic tapping sounded from beyond the room. Vera's eyes went wide. She grabbed a gun and strode out. I sat up. That's when I realized I was dressed in loose cotton trousers and a shirt—neither of which was mine. My head was still pounding, but I had to see what was going on. I crept over to the doorway and poked my head through. The next area was a long, dark corridor with a series of doorways. An underground stream trickled down a groove in the far wall and escaped through a hole in the corner. How smart that was, to choose an underground spot because of its built-in water system. Maybe this hospital was close to the creek that Martina and I had nearly drowned in.

At one end of the long corridor was a set of steep log-and-dirt stairs leading up into a tunnel. A patch of light and a whoosh of winter air streamed from above.

As I watched, the heels of Vera's *postoly* appeared from the tunnel. She was walking slowly down, backward, her ankles trembling to keep balanced. A moment later, I understood why. Her hands clutched one end of a makeshift stretcher. When she was nearly all the way down the steps, the other end of the stretcher became visible. Gripping that end was the kind-eyed soldier who had rescued Martina. On the stretcher was the brown-haired soldier who had saved me. His face was still.

I scrambled back to my cot and lay down, expecting them to bring the injured soldier into this room and lay him on the fourth cot, but when they didn't, I listened, trying to figure out what was going on.

Five minutes. Nothing.

I crept back out. No one was in the corridor. No light or air came through the door at the top of the stairs. I tiptoed over and looked up the tall steps—the door was closed and bolted.

I was about to go back to my room, when I noticed light coming from one of the doorways along the corridor. I stepped quietly past my own door and poked my head through the lit one. An operating room! Kerosene lanterns that were strung from above cast the room in a bright yellow light. A man whose eyes looked bruised with fatigue worked frantically to cut through the fabric of the soldier's pant leg with a large pair of scissors.

"I'll assist as soon as I let Danylo back out," said Vera, hurrying out the door.

The medic looked up and saw me. "You," he said in Ukrainian. "If you're conscious enough to stand there and gawk, you can help." He jerked his head toward a tray of instruments. "Get some scissors. Help me cut these pants off before this man bleeds to death."

I grabbed a pair of sewing shears and stared at them for a moment, my mind filling with the memory of my mother sitting in a comfortable chair before the war, snipping off the frayed bits from the cuff of Tato's dress shirt with scissors just like these.

"Don't just stand there," said the medic. "Help me." He mumbled something under his breath in Yiddish.

Now I was truly confused. Who were these people and which side were they working for?

I stepped quickly over to the injured soldier to see how

I could help. The medic had cut away the pant leg from the bottom to the knee, but was having difficulty ripping it open the rest of the way. I held the scissors in my armpit and reached over to loosen the man's belt buckle. Once it was open, I was able to snip through the heavy waistband and the triple layer of material around the pocket until the entire leg was exposed. At first it was difficult to see where the injury was, there was so much blood, but Vera came back with water. She poured it over the area, washing away blood and exposing a deep black hole in the man's thigh muscle.

"I'm glad to see you haven't fainted yet," the medic told me. "Vera, give the boy the water. He can irrigate while you assist me."

If I'd had something in my stomach, I might have thrown up as Vera held the wound open with metal instruments and the man dug around with surgical forceps, looking for the bullet. Thank goodness the soldier was unconscious. I poured bits of water, making sure those two could see what they were doing. My head throbbed and I felt like I would faint, but I breathed slowly and concentrated on what needed to be done.

"Got it!" said the medic, triumphantly holding up a bullet glistening with blood. "No surprise, a German bullet."

Vera smiled, then reached for a needle and thread. "I'll take over," she said, giving the wounded area a swab of antiseptic.

"Now we keep it dry," said the medic, handing me a wad of gauze.

The two of us kept on blotting away blood as Vera stitched, first the deepest layer of muscle, then the next. I watched her deft movements and steady hands.

An image of Lida flashed into my mind, needle and thread poised, eyebrows crinkled in concentration. Her skillful fingers had earned her one of the safer jobs at the work camp. Was she still safe? I could only hope ... I shook my head and her image disappeared.

When the wound was fully closed up, the medic wrapped it with tape and gauze.

"Stefan was very fortunate that the bullet didn't shatter the bone," he said, wiping sweat off his own brow with a clean rag. He turned to me and held out his hand. "You can call me Abraham," he said. "Surgeon with the Ukrainian Red Cross."

The Ukrainian Red Cross! It was separate from the Soviet one and separate from the German one. I knew that for certain because there was an active chapter in Kyiv during both occupations—Soviet and Nazi. These people were not working for the Germans. They wouldn't care if Martina and I were escaped slaves.

"And what should we call you?" asked Abraham, almost as if he had read my mind.

I shook his hand firmly. Should I use a made-up name or my own? I told him he could call me Luka.

"So you survived the trek—through the borderlands, I take it?—all the way to the mountains," said Abraham. "Luck was on your side."

"Perhaps a little bit of skill as well," said Vera. "When I was unpacking his knapsack, I found things that showed me he knew how to survive in the forest—dried puffball mushrooms, wild foods."

At first I felt a twinge of anger that Vera had searched through my knapsack without my permission, but I couldn't very well stay annoyed. Martina and I were strangers to her, yet Vera had saved our lives at the risk of her own. She was within her rights to minimize any risk to this location—even if that meant searching through my private things.

"Is your friend Czech?" she asked.

"Yes," I said. "How did you know?"

"She was talking in her sleep a few hours ago, and I was fairly certain the language was Czech."

"The Nazis burned her village down," I told Vera. "Most of the people were killed, but she was able to escape."

Vera sat down and didn't say anything for a minute or more, then she brushed a tear from her cheek with the back of her hand.

"She's a lucky one, then," said Vera. "The Nazis have burned the Ukrainian and Polish villages around here as well. They usually take the young children as forced workers. It is a miracle your friend survived."

"And we are fortunate to have you here," Abraham added. "Thank you for your help."

"My father was a pharmacist in Kyiv."

"He's taught you well," said Abraham. Then he and Vera lifted Stefan off the operating table and carried him into the room where Martina and the blond German soldier still rested. I stayed in the operating room and put things in order.

"Come," said Vera, poking her head back into the room. "I've got some soup heating."

I followed her and Abraham down the dark corridor and through yet another doorway. Vera ladled meaty soup into three bowls and passed one of them to me.

"Wild sorrel and rabbit," said Abraham, blowing on his spoon. "Much better than our usual bean, potato, and sorrel soup."

"What are your plans, once you leave here?" asked Vera, stirring her soup.

"I need to get to Kyiv," I said. "That's where I'm from."

"You can't get to Kyiv, Luka," said Abraham.

I swallowed down a spoonful of soup in angry silence, wanting to shout at him that he was wrong. "My plan was to hide out in the mountains until the war was over," I said. "I had no idea that the war would find its way here."

Vera chewed on a bit of meat, then said, "So you're hoping the Soviets will win?"

The image of my grandfather in the mass grave at Bykivnia filled my mind. I thought of my father in a work camp in Siberia. Both were victims of the Soviets. But David and his mother were Nazi victims, killed at Babyn Yar. Lida and Mama and I were all forced laborers— *Ostarbeiters*—thanks to the Nazis. No matter *who* won, *we* all lost. I set the spoon down with a clatter. How could I respond to *that* question?

There was a shuffling of footsteps in the corridor. Abraham hurried out the door. A few moments later he came back, the blond German soldier in tow. "Guess who's woken up?"

The soldier seemed in awe of his surroundings. "What is this place?" he asked.

"You can tell your superiors that your life was saved by

the Ukrainian Insurgent Army," said Vera, replying to him in German so he could understand. "We shall be keeping your weapons, but you go free."

She rooted around in her pocket, pulled out a pamphlet with German printing on it, and shoved it into his hand. "You can share that with your fellow soldiers," she said. "It explains who we are." Then she took out a bandanna and a rope. "Sorry, but we're going to have to restrain you and cover your eyes before we release you."

The soldier's eyebrows lifted. I was surprised as well.

She stood up and dangled the rope. The soldier shoved the pamphlet into a pocket and held out his hands. He did not protest as she tied his wrists together, then wrapped the cloth around his eyes and knotted it. She placed her hands on his shoulders and directed him toward the steps. While she was doing this, Abraham shrugged on a heavy coat and slipped his feet into winter boots.

I watched as the two of them got the soldier outside, then Vera came back down alone. I stood with her at the foot of the stairs as she waited for Abraham to come back.

I wanted to ask her about this—their taking in a Nazi soldier, treating him, then releasing him—but her expression was so focused, I kept silent.

After long minutes of waiting, there was a faint rhythmic tapping from above. Vera took out her pistol and walked up the stairs. Moments later she came back down, Abraham two steps behind her, his cheeks red from cold. He kicked his boots off and hung up his coat. "Let's finish our soup," he said. "Who knows when the next patient will arrive."

The soup had cooled, but it filled my stomach. "You can't have taken him very far away," I said to Abraham. "Aren't you afraid that others will follow you here?"

"We work on a relay system," said Abraham. "I only had to get him to the first perimeter of scouts. Even most of our own soldiers don't know exactly where this hideout is."

Vera looked over at me. "Just before we were interrupted, Luka, you said that you wanted to get back to Kyiv. Do you still have family there?"

"My mother and I were both taken to Germany as *Ostarbeiters*," I said. "Before that, the Soviets shot my grandfather. But they took my father to Siberia and he could still be alive. If he is, he'll go back to Kyiv, looking for me and Mama. If I don't get back there, we'll never be a family again."

"The Germans were driven out of Kyiv a few days ago," said Vera. "But our sources say that the fighting is still very heavy all around there. If you try to go to Kyiv, you will be killed."

"I am not a coward who runs away from danger," I

said, setting my spoon down with a clatter. "I got all the way here without being caught. I'll sneak into Kyiv."

Vera didn't answer. Instead, she put a large spoonful of soup into her mouth and chewed it thoughtfully. I saw her exchange a glance with Abraham. After a long moment of silence, she looked at me and said, "I cannot stop you from killing yourself, but if you truly want to see your father someday, you cannot get to Kyiv right now."

"And your father isn't *in* Kyiv, Luka," said Abraham in a gentle voice. "Do you really think Stalin would let prisoners out of Siberia in the middle of the war and send them back home? Think with your brain, boy, not with your heart."

My fists clenched at his words. Was he calling me stupid? I took a deep breath and let it out slowly, trying to make myself calm. I had been thinking clearly, hadn't I? In my heart I knew that Tato was still alive. My brain knew it too. I had to get to him. We had to be a family again. We'd been separated too long as it was.

Family . . .

All at once, an overwhelming sadness washed over me. Much as I hated to admit it, what Vera and Abraham said had a ring of truth to it. All this time, I had placed my hopes on getting away from the war, getting to Kyiv. Finding my father. But how could I deny the facts that were in front of me? Now I had to admit that it was impossible to walk away from a war that was so huge. Getting to Tato would have to wait—*again*!

I felt utterly lost. Reaching my father looked impossible right now. I held my head in my hands. This was too much to take in all at once.

"What am I supposed to do, then?" I said it out loud, as much to myself as to Abraham and Vera. "I'm not going to give up."

"No one is suggesting that you give up, Luka," said Vera. "You just have to wait until the time is right."

I felt like a complete failure, powerless to help the people I loved. I hadn't stopped David from being killed, and I had left Lida at the camp . . . even if she had wanted me to escape. I should have stayed so I could protect her. I hadn't rescued my mother. Now I couldn't get back to my father.

I raised my head from my hands and looked at Vera. Her eyes were shadowed with fatigue and there was a line of worry on each side of her mouth. She wasn't searching for her own family right now. She was helping a bigger family—fighting for the freedom of her country.

I glanced at Abraham. He too looked like he was about to collapse from the weight of the world. Yet the two of them kept on fighting—for freedom, for all the people who were being killed by the Soviets and the Nazis.

I couldn't get to my father right now, and I couldn't help Lida or my mother. But I *could* fight for freedom. That's what Tato would do.

"I want to join your underground army."

Abraham and Vera were silent, but as I watched them, it was like they were having a conversation with their eyes. Abraham nodded slightly, then Vera said, "It's time for you to rest."

CHAPTER SEVENTEEN
BLINDFOLD

When I got back to the recovery room, Martina's eyes were open, but she didn't look completely awake. I sat on the edge of her bed.

"Luka," she said, her eyes focusing on my bandage. "Thank goodness you're okay."

"I'm doing better than you," I said. "All I've got is a cut on my head, but you've got frostbitten toes and all those stitches on your cheek."

Her hand flew up to her face and she gingerly felt the train track of stitches. "I don't remember how I did that." She looked at her bandaged feet, then wiggled her toes. "One big toe is achy, and the other toes feel tingly and hot, but I can *feel* all of them."

What a relief. We had done everything we could to keep our feet from freezing these last weeks, but Martina's *postoly* had made it almost impossible.

She propped herself up and looked at the cot that now held a sleeping Stefan. "He looks familiar," she said.

"He's the one who brought you here, wrapped up in his coat. A second soldier rescued me."

"Are we under the *ground*?" Martina asked, looking around at the tall wooden walls and bits of sunlight filtering through the narrow slits high above.

"We are. This whole hospital is hidden underground."

Vera stepped into the room just then and went over to Martina's cot. In one hand was a bowl of soup, and in the other a pamphlet similar to the one that the German soldier had been given, but I could see that this one was in Ukrainian.

"I'm glad you're awake," she said. "Call me Vera. I'm a doctor with the Ukrainian Red Cross. And what should we call you?"

"My name is Martina."

"It is good to meet you," said Vera. "I'm sure you're hungry." She set the bowl and a spoon into Martina's hands, then turned and gave me the paper. "Here's something for you both to read. It's about our army."

As Martina ate the soup, I told her about the German soldier who had been treated and released, and what I had found out so far about the people who called themselves

Vera and Abraham, and the army they were assisting. I opened the pamphlet and read silently.

"What does it say?" asked Martina.

"Give me a minute to read it through and then I'll summarize."

Martina nodded and ate more soup.

The pamphlet was entitled *What Is the Ukrainian Insurgent Army Fighting For?* It was dated August 1943.

I scanned the first page, then said, "The Ukrainian Insurgent Army—also called the UPA—is fighting against the Nazis *and* the Soviets."

"But what are they fighting *for?*" asked Martina.

I flipped the page. "It says they want equality for all citizens, regardless of age, sex, religion, or nationality."

"And this hospital serves the UPA?" Martina asked.

I looked over at Vera. She nodded.

"Then I want to join," Martina said. "My father was in the Czech Underground when he was killed. They had ideas like this."

"My father ended up in Siberia because of ideas like this," I said.

Vera leaned forward on the edge of one of the empty cots. "Our groups protect children in villages from both Nazi and Soviet attacks, but many children help us," she said. "Not in the army, but in the villages. You and Luka could be trained to help."

"It would be better than running and hiding," said Martina.

"As long as you're willing to stand up to Stalin and Hitler, you can work with us," Vera said. "Besides, if you survived in the forests for so long, you must have a number of skills."

We stayed in the underground bunker just long enough to ensure that Martina's feet would heal. She was not used to being idle, so she limped around, doing small chores—making soups and herbal teas, keeping the kitchen spotless—while I assisted with medical help.

Once, after helping set a broken arm, I walked into the kitchen and saw Martina lost in concentration as she stirred a pot of rabbit stew. A sudden image of Lida appeared in my mind, shoulders bent with fatigue and a bowl of watery turnip soup in front of her. Was she safe in the labor camp, or should I have tried against all odds to take her with me? Lida was strong and resourceful. I could only hope that she also had luck on her side.

Martina looked up at me and smiled. The image of Lida faded. "You look like you've seen a ghost," she said.

I hope not, I said to myself.

Over the weeks, a steady stream of injured soldiers was brought in to the hospital. They were always blindfolded, whether they were Red Army or Wehrmacht. Even most of the UPA soldiers were blindfolded.

"Why do you blindfold your own soldiers?" I asked Abraham one day as I helped him clean the surgical room after he'd put back together a Red Army soldier's shredded hand. "You're on the same side."

Abraham wiped off the last splatter of blood from the operating table, then cleaned the whole thing down with disinfectant. "What if a UPA soldier were captured?" he asked. "He could be tortured into giving up this location. What they don't know cannot be revealed."

"Has that happened before?"

Abraham pointed up to the ceiling. "See those openings? Nazis and Soviets have destroyed underground hospitals by sending poison gas through those. Or by lobbing grenades through the hatch—you name it. It's essential that our locations stay secret."

Just then Vera's head poked through the doorway. "I have a surprise for Martina," she said, holding out a bundle.

Martina limped over and looked at it. "What do you have there?"

147

"Open it."

Martina worked open the rope and pulled out the contents—a pair of sturdy leather boots that looked brand-new, heavy wool socks, gloves, a hat. The leather bundle they had been wrapped in was a sheepskin-lined winter coat. As she held each item, I thought of Lida, who had no shoes, no socks, no warm coat. I was happy for Martina's good fortune, but how I wished I could snatch those boots and somehow get them to Lida.

"Thank you," said Martina, grinning.

"You'll be needing them," said Vera. "Once it's dark, you and Luka will be leaving."

CHAPTER EIGHTEEN
INTO THE MOUNTAINS

The last thing I saw was Abraham tying a bandanna across Martina's eyes. A piece of cloth fell over my own eyes and a knot was tied snugly at the back of my head.

"Will you be tying our hands as well?" I asked.

"No need," said Vera. She went up the narrow steps first, and Martina followed, her hands on Vera's hips for guidance. I followed behind, my hands clutching Martina's belt. I had a vision of one person taking a wrong step and all of us tumbling down in a tangled clump.

We paused at the top and I heard the sound of metal scraping metal—likely Vera unlocking the hatch. We took a few more steps up.

"Stop!" Vera said. "I need to show you exactly where to place your feet. First, Martina."

I let go of Martina's belt and listened to the footsteps.

"Now you," said Vera. She grabbed one pant leg and guided me to skip the top step, then to angle my foot in a certain way. "Good," she said, once I was completely out. "The top step is booby-trapped with explosives, as is the ground around the entrance, to protect us from intruders."

"I'll take them from here," said a gruff voice that seemed somehow familiar. Was it Danylo?

"Can we take the bandannas off now?" Martina asked.

"Not yet," said the voice. "But you'll be able to do that soon, maybe fifteen minutes. We'll go in single file so that we don't make a triple set of footsteps in the snow. Martina, hold the back of my belt. Luka, hold on to Martina."

In this awkward caterpillar fashion, we stumbled over what must have been rocks and logs. We slipped on ice and slush and even leaves, and my arms and neck ached. It seemed much longer than fifteen minutes.

All at once a gust of wind cooled my face. I blinked. The bandanna had been whisked off. But I still couldn't see much in the pitch-darkness.

"This way," whispered Danylo. "We've got to make ten kilometers before dawn."

As we walked, my eyes slowly adjusted to the darkness, and my feet got into the rhythm. When Martina and I had made our long trek, we often covered long distances—even twenty kilometers on a very good night—but this journey was through treacherous and steep ground. We were walking up a mountain, after all. Added to that, Danylo had us crisscross and circle in a most confusing fashion, so each kilometer felt like ten.

"We can't avoid the footprints in this snow," said Danylo under his breath. "All we can do is camouflage the direction."

Martina's stamina surprised me. She managed to keep her pace even in her brand-new boots. I felt light-headed but didn't want to hold us up, so I put one foot in front of the other and kept on going.

Just as sunlight appeared overhead, the trees began to thin and we neared a thatched cottage. An older woman wearing an embroidered shirt and a long skirt under her sheepskin vest stepped out the door. In her hands was a rifle, but her face broke out into a smile when she recognized Danylo.

"Ulana," he said. "Good to see you. Has there been any trouble?"

She shook her head. "Come inside. We'll talk."

The cottage was warm and smelled of baking bread. A table with a stack of plates, some cups, and a pitcher of water dominated the room. It also held a map, some pencils, and paper. The place seemed like a meeting area, not just a regular cottage. A girl wearing a gun belt set a steaming loaf of bread on the table.

"Danylo, you and your friends are welcome. Sit," said Ulana, propping her rifle close to the door. "You're just in time for some of Orysia's fresh bread."

We slipped off our boots and coats and sat at the table. Orysia pulled off hunks of bread for each of us and set out a container of soft goat cheese. As we ate, Danylo asked Ulana, "What's been happening?"

"The Germans still don't know where our camp is," said Ulana. "But they're all over the area."

Danylo turned to me and Martina. "Finish your bread. We've got to get moving."

We walked a few kilometers farther down a fairly broad mountain road. Along the way, we encountered a series of armed sentries, some wearing the familiar assortment of Soviet and German uniforms with the insignia removed, and others in regular peasant clothing. Even though I was on the alert, these soldiers were so good at hiding that I didn't spot them until they stepped in front of us, weapons poised. But they would lower their weapons at the sight of Danylo and let us pass.

We kept on walking, meeting more sentries along the way. A few kilometers farther, we reached an open area cleverly concealed within tall fir trees. Half-hidden here and there was a series of plain wooden buildings, their roofs and sides camouflaged with mud and fir boughs. As we got closer, I was astounded by the sheer number of hidden buildings.

Our way was blocked by armed guards, and this time, even though their faces showed that they recognized Danylo, that alone was not enough to get us through.

"Password," one demanded. He looked no older than me, his rifle at the ready.

"*Colibri*," said Danylo.

The young guard lowered his rifle. "You can go through."

An officer stepped out of one of the buildings and grinned when he saw Danylo. When he looked at me and Martina, the smile disappeared. "Are these two here to help, or are they homeless locals?"

"They want to help, Bohdan, and they're good ones," said Danylo. "Martina is swift and quiet." Then he pointed to me. "Luka here apprenticed under his father—a pharmacist."

"You've got to do weapons training first," Bohdan said. "So let's get started."

We walked up a hill, and beyond was a clearing with two teenage boys and a girl, all in regular clothing, standing at attention and facing an instructor. On a table in front of the instructor was an array of weapons—two different kinds of machine guns, automatic pistols, and a variety of rifles.

"Sofia, Roman, and Viktor, choose a weapon," the instructor said. "They're not loaded. Your first job is to disassemble your weapon. Pay close attention, because your next job will be to put it back together."

Once the trainees were busy with their tasks, the instructor greeted Danylo. "Are these two new ones for me?"

"Yes," said Danylo.

"Pick a weapon, each of you," said the instructor. "And get to work."

"Stand up a bit straighter," said Martina. "And rest the buttstock closer to the middle of your chest."

It felt like such an unnatural way to position the rifle. Why was it so easy for Martina? She was the top shooter in our group—unlike me. I lined up the little notch at the end of the barrel so it was exactly in the middle of the notched rear sight, and slowly began to squeeze the trigger.

"Focus on the center circle of the paper target, not the front sight on the rifle," said Martina.

I loosened my finger from the trigger and glared at her.

She stuck her tongue out at me. "You're going to miss that haystack completely if you don't calm down," she said.

Calm down? How was I supposed to do that with her hovering over me and second-guessing everything I did? I didn't say that to her, though. Instead, I ignored her. I tightened my index finger over the trigger, then *bang*. I practically fell over from the impact of the recoil.

"Congratulations," said Martina. "You managed to hit the haystack this time."

"Where?"

"The top corner," she said, pointing. "See where the paper's fluttering a little bit?"

"I did everything right," I muttered, pointing the barrel of the semiautomatic to the ground for safety. "I should have hit the bull's-eye."

"You can't be good at everything," said Martina, reaching for the rifle butt.

"I can't shoot like you. I can't track quietly like you. I feel useless."

"Stand over there," Martina said, indicating a spot beside a scrawny fir tree. "You're making *me* nervous."

"People aren't going to stand away from me in a combat situation," I said. "I've got to get used to firing a rifle under all sorts of circumstances."

Martina rolled her eyes. "Fine," she said. "Stand wherever you want."

In one smooth, quick motion she took her stance, aimed, and shot. And hit the center of the target. Then she angled the rifle to the ground. "I can shoot and track, Luka, but you can heal people. I wish I could do that."

We walked back to the main part of the camp together, savoring the rare bit of free time. We had finished our training the day before and were ready to work.

Petro, the instructor, was not happy with my rifle skills. "You'll be a village medic," he told me. "But if Martina can get your shooting up to par, I'll let you carry a gun."

"I want to fight for my country, just like you," I told him.

He shook his head at that. "Be careful what you wish for," he said. "And go get some sleep."

Lida brushes my cheek with a prickly frond of a fir branch. "Can you hear them?"

"Hear what?" I ask, wrapping my fingers around her narrow wrist so she can't tickle me anymore.

"The bullets that I made for the Nazis . . ."

Hot bile forms in my stomach. Surely Officer Schmidt wouldn't send someone as young as her to the munitions factory? Lida had to be working at the laundry, not at the—

"Now, Luka! Get up!" The dream was achingly real. But not as real as the shouting.

I opened my eyes. Not Lida, but Martina, with Roman by her side.

She shoved away the fir branches that covered our sleeping pit and pulled me by the hand with such force I thought she'd tear my arm off. Sofia darted out. Viktor too. And then I heard the growling of an airplane up above.

I scrambled to my feet, grabbing my rifle and making sure my medic bag was securely strapped to my waist.

The growl got louder. I looked into the sky. A Soviet plane was terrifyingly close . . .

"Take your positions," shouted Martina.

The plane circled away, then came back in a wide arc. We lined up and aimed. It flew away without firing.

"Guns down," said Martina.

"It's strange," said Petro when the group assembled in the main camp after the plane had disappeared. "Why would a single Soviet plane fly overhead?"

I wondered the same thing too. It seemed almost spooky.

CHAPTER NINETEEN
ZHURAKI

Our group was assigned to the defense of Roman and Viktor's village of Zhuraki, which was at the foot of our mountain just off the main roadway. For me, this was a letdown. I wanted to be in the middle of battle, to be a hero.

Instead, I was stuck in this sleepy little village of old people and children. I understood why they needed protection. Almost all of the fighting-age men had already been killed or taken away by one side or the other. The women were mostly gone too—probably forced laborers in Germany. And the war zone was close by. Right now, Zhuraki was in German-held territory, but that could change any day.

The only men of fighting age left in the village besides Roman and Viktor was Oleh, who had a dislocated shoulder, and Pavlo. They took shifts with us to defend Zhuraki.

On a bitterly cold Sunday morning, I stood on guard with my feet turning to blocks of ice as I listened to the bells of Zhuraki call the villagers to church. I would have loved to set down my rifle and stand among them, not just to listen to the service but to get warm. Instead, I stomped my feet and shivered.

"Our shift will be over soon," said Martina, her lips blue with cold.

Viktor's teeth chattered as he paced back and forth in front of the village entrance.

Sudden running footsteps. The blur of a uniform. A sharp crack to the back of my head. I fell to the snow. Smoke. Pounding. Muffled screams.

I bolted up to a sitting position, but almost fell back down again from wooziness. I must have been knocked out. But for how long?

I took a deep breath and tried to get to my feet. Something was very wrong.

Martina lay on her back, her eyes closed and a trickle of blood coming from her ear. Viktor was curled into a ball, whimpering, a mottled bruise forming on his jaw. I felt the tender spot on the back of my head. It was soft and pulpy and my fingertips came away slick with blood. Who had attacked us?

The smoke!

Flames licked up the sides of the church, billows of black smoke above the spire. Muffled screaming and pounding.

"Viktor! Martina!" I shouted. "The church. We've got to help them!"

Martina's eyes opened. Viktor sat up. I ran to the flaming church, Viktor stumbling a few steps behind me.

Someone had wedged a thick piece of wood through the brass handles, so no matter how hard the people pushed from inside, the doors wouldn't open. I grabbed one end of the wood and pulled. It didn't budge. Viktor gripped the other end and we rocked it back and forth until it split apart.

The door burst open with the weight of many bodies. People fell on top of each other, their backs alight with flames, screaming. I grabbed on to a girl who had collapsed on top of another, and helped her to her feet. She stumbled out of the church in a daze. The woman beneath her cradled a young boy. She ran out, weeping hysterically, the boy's eyes wide with fear. An elderly man dashed out, his hair alight and his jacket in flames. He threw himself down into a snowbank and rolled, putting out the fire.

I didn't stop to consider exactly what must have happened. All I wanted to do was concentrate on saving as many people as we could. But as we pulled more people out, I realized that many were already dead—not from the fire but from breathing in the smoke. Viktor let out a long, howling cry when he recognized the familiar form of his own mother amidst a crush of corpses.

Martina ran up to us, out of breath. "Water!" she ordered, rushing out again. "You and you"—she pointed to the girl and woman—"get buckets. Start pumping."

But the church was old and wooden, and buckets of water were no match for the roaring flames. We doused the cottages closest to the church to contain the fire and hoped for the best.

It wasn't until the following day, when we did a count of the living and dead, that we realized Oleh and Pavlo were both missing.

"How did it start?" I asked a girl named Sonya as I put ointment on her burned palms.

"There was a crash through the high window and a ball of fire burst in," she said. "Oleh and Pavlo bolted out to catch the person who did it. But then we heard shouts in German . . . shots . . . banging at the door.

"I tried to push the doors open. They wouldn't budge. A second ball of fire crashed through a window. Flames— so many flames. People coughing. The smoke. Some were heaving at the door and screaming. It was horrible." Sonya's voice trembled.

"Pavlo and Oleh—I wonder where they are."

Sonya sighed. "Probably taken to the death camp hidden in the woods. We've heard about it, but no one knows where it is."

I felt like it was my fault that the fire began and my fault that Pavlo and Oleh had been captured. How could we have let ourselves be knocked unconscious? What kind of self-defense unit were we?

"We need to search the area," I said to Viktor a few moments later. "Maybe we can figure out where the death camp is."

The initial footprints were easy to track—signs of a scuffle, and dragging footsteps in the snow. We followed the tracks out of the village and down the road until they became impossible to separate from all the other footprints and markings made by the German and Soviet troops.

"There was a truck here very recently," said Viktor, nudging fresh tire tracks in the snowy mud.

Keeping ourselves hidden behind trees and snow, we traced the path of a truck a couple of kilometers down the road. It led to an encampment of German soldiers, but there were no prisoners that we could see.

We spent the rest of the day and into the night combing the area, looking for clues about where the camp might be. It was an exhausting and cold job, but I was determined to find Pavlo and Oleh. The fact that Viktor was from the area helped a little bit, but it was hard work searching for clues while staying hidden ourselves.

"Do you really think we'll ever find the camp?" I asked Viktor, sitting down on the stump of a dead tree and holding my head in my hands. We had searched all through the night, and the morning light was just appearing. "This seems to be an impossible task."

He slumped down beside me. For a long time he didn't say anything. Then he sat up straight. He pointed to a rutted mud track through the trees that was partly hidden by clumps of snow and leaves. In the darkness, we had missed it. "That's new," he said.

The track led a few hundred meters into the woods. We didn't walk on the road itself but through the trees, with the track in view. Finally we spotted an outpost manned by two German soldiers with submachine guns blocking the track.

We stayed hidden behind a tree, hoping that they wouldn't see us. After several tense minutes, I poked my head out to see what they were doing. They were looking in the other direction. I motioned to Viktor and we silently moved a meter or so farther in, then hid behind some brush. We waited a few more minutes, then repeated the action. Slowly, carefully, we timed our movements through the woods to when they were looking the other way.

Half a kilometer past the outpost, a subtle whiff of decay tinged the air, but we kept going forward.

"Stop," whispered Viktor, putting his arm out in front of me. "Look through those trees."

In the midst of this vast wilderness was a well-hidden barbed-wire enclosure with watchtowers camouflaged within the trees, manned by armed guards. It was an open-air prison, filled with emaciated civilians—mostly men, but some women as well. There was nothing to shelter them from snow and wind, so they huddled together in clusters for warmth. Among them I spotted a man with a sling whose clothes were not as ragged. It was Oleh. But for many of the others, it was too late. Just outside of the enclosure was a mound of frozen corpses.

I forced myself to breathe slowly, think clearly, and stay hidden. The regular German army wouldn't have a prison like this, would they? It would have to be the Gestapo—trained murderers. And they'd need to have administrative buildings close by. I climbed onto higher ground. From this vantage point I could see beyond the prison to a cluster of newly built barracks a hundred or so meters away. Were these the offices and sleeping quarters for the staff? I memorized the locations of the buildings.

"We've got to tell Petro that we found this place," I whispered to Viktor.

Just then one of the sentries in the watchtower turned our way. If he'd looked hard, he would have seen me for sure. I stood still and waited for him to turn away.

It was tricky for us to steal away, and it didn't help that I still had a raging headache from yesterday's blow to my head. Viktor had to feel even worse. He had lost his mother and so many friends and neighbors. And now seeing a mound of corpses being regarded as so much garbage. How could anyone treat another human this way? I couldn't get that stack of dead people out of my mind.

We made it back up the mountain and reported what we'd found to Petro.

"Show me on this," he said, rolling out a detailed map of the area on his desk.

I indicated the area where the camp was. "These buildings back there," I said, pointing to a spot on the map. "They look like the ones in my labor camp. I'm fairly certain they're Gestapo administration buildings."

"Most likely," said Petro.

"Why do they bother to capture civilians now?" I asked Petro. "The Germans are supposedly retreating. Doesn't this just slow them down?"

"Military strategy," said Petro. "As the Soviets have

been pushing closer, the retreating Nazis have been destroying everything that they can't take with them and that could be of use to the Soviets—food, any sort of supplies—and people."

I thought back to what had happened in Kyiv as the Soviets fled the oncoming Nazis. They too had destroyed everything. Why was it always the civilians who suffered most in these wars?

An attack was planned for that very night, with me and Viktor as the advance scouts. It made me proud to fight as a soldier this time instead of just passively protecting a village.

First we ambushed the outpost. That was easy. Petro placed one squad along the icy mud track and another at the main road to stop German reinforcements from coming through. Then the rest of us silently encircled the barracks.

UPA soldiers aimed their rifles at the watchtowers. On Petro's signal, they shot the guards, then dashed to the building.

Viktor and I were on their heels. The front door was bolted from the inside, but Petro gave it one strong kick and it caved in. We stepped through the splinters of wood, not bothering with silence, only going for speed. We were in a hallway with doors along either side. Petro motioned for us to swarm the rooms. I entered the first one on the right, Viktor at my side.

I flicked on the light. A man in nightclothes, with shaggy blond hair, had jumped out of bed and was hastily pulling on civilian clothes. "Get out of my way," he shouted in German.

I took in the entire room—the gray Gestapo uniform hanging from a wall hook; half of the room looking simple and clean like a soldier might have it; the other half more like a storage area, with goods stockpiled nearly to the ceiling. A large burlap sack lay on the floor, sausage links spilling out from the top. Leaning up against the side of the sack was a large framed picture of *The Last Supper*. It looked old and precious and must have been stolen from a church—likely the church that had been burned. On the top of a wooden packing crate was a tarnished chalice filled with thin gold wedding bands. The goods had probably been taken from poor villagers.

I felt like vomiting.

I looked at the soldier. In one quick movement he reached beneath his pillow and drew out a pistol. As he aimed it at my head I realized that it was him or me.

I raised my rifle and shot. His chest exploded and he slumped over. I looked at him, then down at my own trembling hand. For all my bravado, I was shocked that I had actually been able to kill a man. I reasoned that his death meant that many innocent people would live, but my conscience didn't buy it. I bent over and threw up on the floor.

"Let's get out of here," said Viktor.

I stood up, wiping vomit from my lips. "Don't tell anyone I did that, okay?"

"I won't."

When it was all over, Viktor and I ran down to the wire enclosure. Petro had already opened the gate and was directing our soldiers to assist the prisoners. Oleh was there, and so was Pavlo. They came out on their own and hugged us in thanks, then went back in and helped us with those who couldn't walk. Viktor and I rigged a makeshift stretcher from fir boughs and carried out one young prisoner between us who told us that his name was Andrij.

"I can walk," he told us. "Help someone else." But then his knees buckled and he fell to the ground. We got him onto our stretcher. I took off my jacket and covered him with it.

Some prisoners had been taken on our soldiers' backs, others carried like babies. Those who needed treatment but couldn't make it to our mountain camp were blind-folded and carried to various field hospitals in the area.

Once all of the prisoners were looked after, Petro ordered two squads to comb through all of the Gestapo buildings to save anything valuable: food, medicine, clothing, but also intelligence reports. This too was carried back to our camp.

On one of the narrow paths up, I was surprised to see the UPA priest, Father Ruslan, coming down. "Why are you going the other way, Father?" I asked.

"To perform the *Panakhyda*, my son," he said.

Andrij sat up on the stretcher. "Please, Father, take me with you. They were my friends, my neighbors. I need to say good-bye."

The priest nodded. "It would be good for you to be able to do that."

We turned the stretcher around and followed the priest back down to the prison camp.

As we approached the abandoned bodies, my stomach boiled in anger. I thought of that Gestapo soldier in his warm bed, surrounded by things that he'd stolen. Such a life of luxury while people just outside his doorstep were dying of hunger and exposure. Did he deserve to die? Certainly. But my stomach was still queasy at the fact that I had been the one to kill him.

Andrij struggled into a standing position, then leaned against Viktor for support.

Father Ruslan took off his knapsack and asked me to hold it. He removed a small stole and put it over his shoulders, then took out his prayer book, the holy water, and a small packet.

"I would have liked to bury all of the dead," said Father Ruslan, "but the ground is frozen." He held up the packet. "This bit of earth will have to do."

I was overcome with sadness by the sight of the pile of mangled bodies. It had been bad enough to kill these people, but to treat their bodies with such disrespect revolted me. And to leave them just outside the barbed wire, to torment their loved ones—it shook me to the core.

I could hear Andrij gulping back a sob. I put my hand on his shoulder and said, "They're not suffering anymore."

We stood behind Father Ruslan as he sang the *Panakhyda* in such a strong and clear voice that I imagined the treetops shaking. He shook his vial over the mound, making sure that the droplets of holy water reached as many of the bodies as were accessible. Together we sang the *Vichnaya Pamyat*—"Eternal Memory." My mind filled with the images of all of the people that I had lost—my grandfather in that mass grave, David and his mother as they marched toward their death with thousands of Kyiv's

Jews. So many others. Too many others. I looked over at Viktor and knew that he was thinking of his mother. Andrij was racked with sobs.

When the hymn finished, we all stood together in silence under the stars. It was customary to kiss the departed as a final gesture. Father Ruslan did not hesitate. He walked up to the obscene mound of frozen flesh and knelt down, kissing the skull of a person at the bottom—an early victim. One by one, we all did the same, saying good-bye to those we had not known in life. The sensation of my lips on a frozen brow is something I will never forget.

Father Ruslan sprinkled the packet of earth over the dead. This was as close to burial as they would get. And then we left.

On the way back, the only sound was our own breathing. The silence was so profound that it felt like an eternity, as if even the wildlife had disappeared. I was filled with a sense of unease.

Andrij still wore my coat, so Viktor and I took turns wearing his jacket. We were both chilled, but the exertion of carrying Andrij provided a bit of warmth.

By the time we got to our camp, I was nearly dead on my feet with exhaustion, but we carried Andrij right into the hospital. I was going to get myself clean and then come back to help, but a doctor who was in the midst of treating an arm injury said, "You there, I need help."

I hurried over.

"You can call me Samuel," said the doctor, who looked like he hadn't slept in days. "I need you to organize blankets for those people from the prison camp, and give them small sips of water. Not too much all at once."

This hospital was large compared to the underground bunker, but every cot was now full. I found the supply closets and pulled out all of the blankets and wrapped the patients one by one as quickly as I could.

Viktor helped me give them sips of tepid water. Getting these people warm and hydrated was just a small part of what they needed, but it was a first step and could mean the difference between life and death. I was determined to do all that I could to help them. By the time each was bundled in a blanket and had been given water, it was almost dawn. I had been on my feet for forty-eight hours.

As I dragged myself out of the hospital, Samuel called out to me. "Your help tonight has been a godsend."

CHAPTER TWENTY
ONE FRONT LEAVES

The spring of 1944 blended into a series of skirmishes, some with the German Gestapo, others with the Soviets.

We saw more Soviet planes fly overhead for apparently no reason, but we finally understood: They were dropping NKVD agents by parachute behind the German lines.

As for the regular German army, entire units stopped fighting and fled. For them, the war was over.

But for those of us in Ukraine, another chapter of the war was just unfolding. Now that they couldn't get the Germans to do their killing, the Soviets sent in special NKVD groups of hardened soldiers to assist the parachutists. They would encircle a village at dawn and order every man, no matter his age or health, to come to the center square. These soldiers knew about the hiding spots and tunnels beneath the villages. They weren't as easily fooled as the Nazis had been. Any men who didn't come out were found and shot as traitors. Those who did come out were forced into the Red Army without weapons or uniforms, and most ended up being killed in their first battle. It was a terrifying time.

The UPA still held the mountains and forests. I did what I could to help what was left of Zhuraki.

The village self-defense units set up a central hospital in Zhuraki and fortified the protection in the villages on either side of it. A large home was emptied, then outfitted with cots, a surgery area, and a supply room, plus a sleeping area for staff in the cellar.

Vera came in as the doctor. Martina and the other young people I trained with were assigned to defense. Because of my experience as a medic, Danylo decided that I would be Vera's assistant. I was frustrated by that at first, stung by the thought that Danylo didn't have faith in my abilities as a soldier, but secretly I was relieved to be healing instead of shooting.

As the weather grew warmer, herbs and wildflowers sprouted in the warming soil. I collected a good supply of herbs and roots. By the end of the summer, I was able to collect poppy pods, which I mashed in honey to make a sleeping potion for patients in extreme pain. With a variety of oils and alcohol, I made up an array of natural medicines. And of course we had a good cache of supplies that the Germans had abandoned during their retreat, including sulfa, morphine, bandages, iodine, tourniquets, and antiseptics. These supplies were more precious than gold.

Lalya, a village girl who was just about my age, would drop by almost every afternoon. She would lean patiently against the doorway of my supply room, watching intently as I sorted out my medicines and supplies.

"Can I help you do that?" she asked.

"I'm sure you have better things to do than to help me with this," I said, straightening out the folds in a piece of gauze and carefully winding it back up.

"I don't," she said. "Baba takes a nap each afternoon. She scoots me out of the house because she says I'm too noisy."

That made me smile. "In that case, I would appreciate help." I handed her my clipboard with a listing and quantity of each item. "Can you read?"

"Of course."

"Put a check mark beside each item as I call it out."

Days would go by with nothing more than a case of scraped shins, but when the NKVD units attacked, we could barely keep up with the injuries. A bullet to the arm or leg was treatable, but a bomb or rocket blast all too frequently meant people coming in needing a limb amputated. Even when we could save the soldiers' lives, without two feet and both hands, their chances of surviving the next attack were slim. Vera and I did what we could, treating their injuries, dulling their pain.

Late one day, a fighter named Ostap was brought in unconscious on a stretcher, his left leg torn up and bloody. "Shrapnel," said the medic. "Lucky it didn't kill him."

Vera injected the man with morphine and we shifted him to the operating table. It took some time to cut away his shredded pant leg and clear away enough of the blood, but finally a peppering of wounds emerged. A person who stepped on a mine died a horrible death, and people nearby could die of shrapnel wounds. Ostap's leg was a mess, but he was fortunate. Vera methodically probed the dozens of punctures. Each time she pulled out a ragged chunk of metal and let it clunk into the bowl, I winced. Finally she stopped.

"There's probably more in there," she said, setting the forceps down on the tray. "But they're imbedded so deep that I'd cause even more damage digging them out."

Ostap woke just as we were finishing up. He looked down at his leg and asked, "Will I be able to walk again?"

"Can you wiggle your toes?" Vera asked.

He grimaced with pain but managed to make one toe wiggle.

"You were extremely lucky," she said, smiling in relief. "You'll be fine, but you need to let those wounds heal."

When I finally collapsed into bed in the root cellar that night, I dreamed again of Lida, hollow-cheeked and barefoot. How did she manage without shoes all winter? Could she wiggle *her* toes?

I tossed and turned and tried to think of something else, but Lida hovered in my dreams . . . *Hands wrapped around an empty soup bowl, hungry eyes staring up at me. The bowl clatters to the ground . . . Now Lida's hands are wrapped around a small shiny bomb. Her eyes close. The bomb slips from her fingers and explodes . . . Shards of metal blast in all directions . . .*

I jolted awake, my head still filled with the image of that exploding bomb. Where would Lida be now? Would they still have need for her sewing skills, or was she making bombs now, like I had been? And then a terrible thought struck me. I had never wondered who made the *Soviet* bombs. Probably slave laborers like me and Lida. Perhaps even my own father.

There was no point in trying to sleep. I threw back my covers and got up, then walked up the stairs to the main floor of the cottage-hospital. I was splashing water on my face when Martina burst in.

"The villages of Mahala and Bilki, just west of us, have

177

been captured by the Soviets," she said breathlessly. "They're probably coming here next. We need to evacuate to the UPA camp in the mountains."

I looked outside and saw that our fighters were already positioned in defense, weapons poised. So it was all in place.

I got on my outdoor clothing, then filled a knapsack with supplies. Vera did the same. Between the two of us, we had the morphine, surgical instruments, and antibiotics—the most precious items. The three trainee medics took bulkier but less critical supplies, like bandaging and bedding.

Danylo came in with people from the self-defense team, including Martina. "Where are your patients?" he asked.

Vera pointed to Ostap, his gauze-covered leg seeping blood. "We've just got one right now, but he needs to be taken on a stretcher."

Danylo gestured to the door. "All of you out. *Now.*"

Two of the older soldiers helped Ostap into a coat, then onto a stretcher. They hurried out after Danylo. Martina shepherded our three medics while Vera did a final check to make sure that nothing important was left behind.

The only villagers left were eighteen women and six children, which included Lalya and her grandmother. The children all walked on their own except Sonya's little sister, Ana. We walked through the village and out by way of the cemetery, into an area of sparse trees that led to the forests. Our fighters lined our way to protect us.

It was a long trek up the mountain, especially with the civilians, as well as Ostap on his stretcher, but we knew the paths like our own backyard. My knapsack was heavy and kept slipping off one shoulder, but I concentrated on the feet of the person in front of me and kept on walking. Vera and I were spaced in between the civilians. Soldiers protected our front and rear.

Once we had passed the first big hill, the trees got thicker and provided a bit more cover for our group. Martina had been walking up at the front with Danylo, but she slowed her pace until she was walking beside me, her rifle resting on one shoulder.

"Why don't you take the knapsack off your back?" Martina asked. "We could each hold onto a strap and carry it between us."

That made me smile. I missed spending time with Martina. "Thanks for the offer, but I'm fine."

We kept on walking and no one fell behind, but we

couldn't hide effectively—too many children and old people for that. We were met by a second battalion of insurgents when we were a kilometer away from the village. They fanned out around us, giving our group—and most importantly, our medical supplies—a second layer of protection.

Just then a loud grinding whine sounded from above. I looked up—the silhouette of a Soviet bomber. All around us, the ground exploded with fire.

CHAPTER TWENTY-ONE
BLACK SMOKE

Lalya got hit with a piece of flaming metal. She ran into the woods, screaming, the back of her coat licked by flames. I was about to run after her, but her grandmother caught up to her and pushed her to the ground, rolling her in the snow. The flames went out. Steam rose from the blackened hole in Lalya's coat, but she appeared unharmed.

Bits of forest all around us burned. We were incredibly fortunate that no one else had been hit.

"Speed up," said Danylo. "We've got to get out of here before the whole forest goes up in flames."

The two men carrying Ostap were replaced with two fresher men. They trotted as they carried him, anxious to get away from the fire. Sonya, two steps in front of me, buckled and fell, but she still clutched on to Ana.

"What happened?" I asked as I helped her to her feet.

She winced. "My ankle. It's twisted."

Martina dashed into the woods and came back a moment later with a sturdy stick. She broke off the side branches, then handed it to Sonya. "Lean on this," she said. "And let me carry Ana."

Martina held the little girl on one hip and we walked on either side of Sonya in case she fell again. We had to step carefully through trees and over rocks, avoiding patches of ice, so I held Sonya's elbow and steadied her when she needed it, but I also noticed that her ankle was ballooning up.

In less than an hour, Martina, Sonya, and I were trailing behind everyone else. The only people behind us were the village fighters who were protecting the rear.

Below us, a huge swath of the forest billowed with black smoke. Another grinding whine came from up above and a Soviet plane swooped low, peppering us with bullets. Martina passed Ana to me, then aimed and fired. Our fighters up ahead shot at the plane too, and bullet holes appeared in its side. It flew past unsteadily, then plunged into the forest and disappeared. Moments later, the spot in the forest where the plane had disappeared burst into flames.

I turned to Martina and was about to congratulate her on the shot, but her face looked oddly pale. Her knees buckled and she fell to the ground. Her chest was wet with blood.

I knelt down beside her, feeling for a pulse. The rest of the group clustered around. "Viktor, Roman, make a stretcher!"

As they assembled two long branches and tied one of our blankets between them, I unbuttoned Martina's jacket. The bullet had hit the right upper chest. I took off my coat and rolled it up like a pillow, then lifted Martina onto the stretcher, propping up her back with my coat. I covered the wound with some cloth and applied pressure, then put her arm in a sling.

Danylo pushed through the cluster around us and grabbed the front of Martina's stretcher. I carried the back end. Vera picked up Ana and walked beside me. "That was quick thinking," she said.

The rest of the trip was a blur. With every step I took, I was plagued with doubt. If Martina hadn't slowed down to walk with me, would she have been shot? I should have been more careful. One thing only was clear to me: If Martina died, it would be my fault.

When we finally reached the first layer of the UPA mountain defense, the men stationed there radioed ahead. Two fresh soldiers took Martina's stretcher from me and Danylo and we ran the last kilometer to the hospital.

Vera had Martina on an operating table soon after we got there. Her bloodied jacket was open and the sling loosened. Her breathing was labored and her lips had turned blue.

"Scrub up and you can assist," said Vera. "She's got a collapsed lung." I swallowed back my anxiety and did what needed to be done, handing Vera instruments one by one. She made a small incision on the side of Martina's rib cage and plunged in a chest tube. Fluid and blood drained out. Martina gulped in air. Her lips slowly turned a faint pink.

Next, Vera explored the wound to find the bullet, and I irrigated the area with sterile saline so she could see what she was doing.

"I think I've got it," she said, withdrawing the long metal cartridge with forceps. "But she has a broken collarbone and maybe a rib."

She bandaged Martina up and immobilized her arm to keep the collarbone straight. I sat by her bedside for the rest of the day and all through the night.

Sometime before dawn, Martina whispered, "Luka? Are you there?" In the semidarkness I could see that her eyes were heavy-lidded but open. "Can you hold me? I'm cold."

I turned on the light to get a better look at her. The wound on her chest had opened up again and her dressing was bright red. There was a trickle of blood at the corner of her lip. I gathered her into my arms and held her close, feeling the warmth of her blood soaking my shirt.

"It's not your fault, Luka," she said.

But it *was* my fault, and I knew it. I fought back my anger and rocked her gently, trying to keep her warm, keep her safe. If only I could have done that before she got hurt.

And now she wouldn't stop bleeding. I knew she couldn't survive it, and from the look in her eyes, Martina understood that as well.

"Get away from here, Luka," whispered Martina. "You need . . . to live. To tell our story. Don't let my death . . . silence the truth."

"Please don't leave me," I murmured, rocking her gently.

But she was already gone.

CHAPTER TWENTY-TWO
ONE WALKING

The death of Martina left me beyond desolate. It was like a part of me had died. The scent of pine resin reminded me of her. Each time I saw a fellow fighter, or the sky, or a Soviet bomber, I thought of her.

The NKVD seemed furious that our villagers had escaped. They set fire to the forest, then circled the area with troops, who shot anyone fleeing. They bombed our mountain, then executed everyone they found.

Even though our mountain encampment was spread over a large area and was mostly hidden by treetops and camouflage, we were all at grave risk. The Soviets seemed intent on killing every one of us.

For months I buried myself in work—not to forget Martina but as a tribute to her. "You are a healer, not a fighter," she'd told me more than once. And with the Soviets pummeling us, I was in constant demand to set broken limbs, stanch blood, and stitch wounds. If only broken hearts could be mended so simply.

I cannot even guess at the number of people I treated over the rest of the year.

Then, as spring of 1945 approached, we got astounding news: The war had ended. Hitler had committed suicide.

I felt like cheering. One less madman, one less crazed empire builder. But there was still Stalin, still the NKVD.

"You are to leave," Petro told me one day. "We will be starting a different kind of fight now."

"But I want to help you," I told him, outraged that he didn't consider me essential.

"You're young, and you'll have a different job," he said. "The UPA will stay and fight to the death, defending our country's right to live in freedom. But if we all die, then who will tell our story? Stalin?" He spat on the ground. "You will bear witness for us, Luka. For all those who have been silenced by death."

Petro's words echoed Martina's own.

"But how will I do that?"

"Get away from here alive. Go west. When the time is right to tell our story, you'll know it."

I thought about Petro's words and I did agree with them, but I had a more immediate goal. If I could no longer fight for my country, the time had come for me to go east, to find my father. I packed up my meager belongings, and before I left for Kyiv, I confronted Petro once more.

"I will tell our story, Petro," I said. "But before I do that, I must go back to Kyiv and find my father."

He gave me a strange look. "Isn't your father in Siberia?"

"He was. But now that the war is over, surely he'll be let out. Kyiv will need pharmacists, and he is one of the best."

"Luka," Petro said, "if only it were that easy." He rested a hand on my shoulder. "It is unlikely that your father is alive. The Siberian camps are as bad as the Nazi concentration camps. Few people manage to survive. And we've had no intelligence reports of prisoners being released."

I crossed my arms. "I cannot simply forget my own father."

"I'm not telling you to forget him, Luka. I'm telling you to wait until the time is right."

"I've served the Underground faithfully," I said. "And I've delayed finding my father for two years. I cannot wait any longer."

"Get a hold of yourself, Luka," Petro said. "We don't always get what we want." He sighed deeply. "There may come a time in the future when you can search for your father. But now . . ." He looked me in the eye. "I have family too," he said. "Do you think I don't understand what you're going through? But right now, it's your duty to stay alive. I've ordered you to be a witness."

More than anything, I felt like punching Petro. I knew what he said was right, but it didn't make it any easier for me to accept. I clenched my hands. "Fine," I said. "I'll go west. For now."

I turned and walked away from him. The first tree I came to I punched hard, bloodying my knuckles.

Who could have foreseen that I would be retracing my route and going back through the mountains and foothills and forests to get back to where I had escaped from?

Petro made sure that I was outfitted with sturdy clothing, and he gave me plenty of food, but he did not give me a gun.

"You're a civilian now," he said. "For you, the war is over. Your brains and heart are all you'll need."

As I trekked back through the now familiar mountains and forests, memories of Martina would catch me off guard. I found myself weeping at the sight of a squirrel or a rushing creek, the sound of rain or a snapping twig. So many memories, all filled with Martina.

When I was well beyond the foothills, I saw another traveler, a young man like me, dressed in homespun. His shoes were held together with rope and his only possession was a small cloth bag slung over his back. I followed behind him as Martina had done with me at first. At night, I'd creep up into a tree close to his encampment and I would breathe in the scent of roasted rabbit. Even though I didn't talk to him, I wondered if he had a sense of me. I would see him stop suddenly sometimes and just listen.

I stayed hidden and watched as he met up with two more travelers—a man and a woman. These weren't mountain people. The man's feet were bloodied and bare and his shirt and trousers hung in shreds. The woman's head was shaven and there was a rip in her shirt where a badge used to be. Had it been an OST badge from a labor camp or a yellow star from a death camp?

The three of them camped together, the first one showing the other two how to snare and cook a rabbit, how to gather berries. As I crouched in the tree above them, my stomach grumbled from the scent of sizzling meat. I had been living on water and dried food. I hadn't wanted to light a fire and give my position away. I swallowed back my hunger and bided my time.

They encountered six more refugees, but I still stayed

hidden. These were different yet again. They were adequately dressed and better fed, and if I had to hazard a guess, I'd say they were ethnic Germans. Unlike the mountain boy with his single cloth bag, or the escapees with nothing, these six carried large sacks filled with food. At night, when the mountain boy started the fire, these Germans drew out cookies and sausage and passed them around. It nearly drove me mad, the scent of so much food.

When they bedded down for the night, I snuck down from my tree and stole three links of sausage. The dry chunks were hard to swallow. I thought of Martina and her taking my biscuits when she was hiding from me.

One thing I learned from following these refugees was that what had been the Reich was now broken up into various zones, each administered by a different Allied nation. The area where Helmut and Margarete's farm had stood was now part of the Soviet zone. I didn't want to go there, and from the sounds of the refugees, none of them wanted to go there either.

There was a large American zone to the southwest of us—just beyond the Czechoslovakian border. That's where they decided to go and I was happy to shadow them.

By May of 1945, the group had swelled to a dozen, but soon there were new clusters of people as well. When it grew to hundreds, there was no point in me still hiding. One day I simply stepped in behind and kept on walking.

We traveled on open roads through Czechoslovakia, through the rubble of bombed buildings and destroyed German tanks and trucks. More people joined us every day. People who had been captives—laborers, prisoners of war, death-camp survivors. Mixed in were escaped Soviet and German soldiers, and civilians. I stayed alone, though I walked with thousands. I listened in on conversations and was struck by the variety of languages. Most I didn't understand, but for the few that I did, the conversations had a theme. Finding loved ones, getting to someplace safe.

Once, while warming my hands over an open fire with many others, I heard a familiar accent peppered in amidst the chatter—a woman's voice—and she had to have come from Kyiv. I looked up and listened, trying to figure out which person the voice had come from. And then I saw her, a bone-thin woman who was nearly bald, although tufts of gray hair sprouted out wildly here and there. She held a potato on a stick over the flames.

I walked around the fire until I was beside her, then crouched down.

She looked at me warily. "I'm not sharing my food."

"I don't want your food."

She looked at me again. "You're from Kyiv too," she said. "I can hear it in your voice."

"I am. But I left long ago. How about you?"

"I was there until the bitter end," she said. "One of the few who actually walked out alive."

"I was thinking of going there," I told her. "To see if I can find my father. He was in Siberia. Or my mother. She was taken as an *Ostarbeiter* to Germany."

The woman studied my face in silence, then looked at her potato, turning it slowly so it would cook evenly. "Your mother would never go back to Kyiv," she stated.

"She would," I said. "My whole family will go back. Otherwise, how will we find each other?"

"The Soviets are running Kyiv now," she said, her eyes still on the potato. "They'd punish your mother for her Nazi sympathies."

Poor woman, the war must have made her mad. "My mother doesn't have Nazi sympathies. She was a *victim* of the Nazis."

"Do you think that matters to Stalin?" said the woman. "He's made it clear: Anyone who survived the Nazi occupation is to be punished for not fighting hard enough." She turned to me then. "Why do you think *I'm* fleeing west?"

"But how will I ever find my father?" I asked.

The look she gave me then was almost motherly. "Who knows?" she said. "But you won't find him in Kyiv."

I didn't entirely believe her but didn't want to argue. I got up, leaving her and her precious potato. Maybe it wasn't possible to go back right this moment, but I wasn't about to give up so easily. For now, I would keep going west. Perhaps I'd find Lida and Mama first, but I'd definitely be going back to be with Tato, even if they said it was dangerous. I couldn't stand the thought of Tato going back home and finding his wife and son missing.

Hordes of ragged people walked along together. There was safety in numbers, that was certain, but there was also misery. The devastation of Martina's country wrung my heart. And it made me wonder what might be left of Kyiv.

After weeks of walking, we arrived at a vast cluster of American army trucks, refugees milling around, soldiers frantically passing out items of food, medics circulating among us to see who needed help.

An American soldier reached into a bag and drew out an orange. "Eat," he said to me, pointing to his mouth.

I had seen oranges in the display window at the special grocery store in Kyiv, where high-ranking party members shopped, but I had never tasted one. I was overwhelmed by this soldier's generosity. I took a huge bite and nearly gagged.

The soldier shook his head, took out another orange and bit into it just like I had, but then spat that small part out. He dug his thumbs into the hole he'd made and pulled back the skin. Then he popped a chunk from inside the orange into his mouth. I did the same. It was so tasty that I sat right down and devoured the rest of it.

The American soldiers were trying to get all of us refugees into lineups. I walked up and down to figure out what was going on. At the front of the line was a series of desks, each with an American officer ready with pen and paper. Each officer had an interpreter; beyond that was a closed-in area with more refugees milling around.

I got into the line of people speaking Ukrainian, then waited for hours until it was my turn, still thinking of that orange.

"Where are you from?" the interpreter asked me in Ukrainian.

"Kyiv."

"Your name?"

"Luka Barukovich."

The officer wrote that down.

"Age?"

"Thirteen."

"What did you do in the war?"

I was about to tell him about the UPA, but then I stopped. The Soviet Union was an Allied nation. Did this American soldier share information with the Soviets? What about the interpreter? Everything I did during the war would be regarded with suspicion by the Soviets, so I erred on the side of caution and answered with part of the truth. "I was in a work camp."

The interpreter said something to the officer in English. Then the officer stamped a paper and handed it to me. "Go through."

CHAPTER TWENTY-THREE
SAFETY

Once I stepped beyond the partition, they made me strip and have a shower, then dusted me with lice powder. That brought back strong memories of my first day at the work camp with Lida, but this time when I came out, there was a set of soft new clothing for me to wear, and a pair of shoes that actually fit. It felt so good to be clean.

It was safe in the displaced persons camp, and there was food—plenty of it, although it was sometimes strange. The Americans had quite a challenge feeding so many people, so we'd have baked beans for days on end, then other times warmed-up beef stew out of cans, then maybe nothing but bread and cheese. It didn't bother me. After so much hunger over so many years, I could have eaten a well-salted shoe.

The medics were having trouble keeping up with all of the refugees' problems, mostly malnutrition, eye diseases, lung infections. But they also had to protect against things like cholera and typhus. Through an interpreter, I offered my help, but the Red Cross nurse just smiled. "We are here to help *you*."

That same nurse came up to me later as I leaned against a demolished truck, eating a piece of white bread. "Family. Find?" she asked, mispronouncing the Ukrainian words.

I had no idea what she was trying to tell me. She took me by the elbow and guided me to a different Red Cross building. Another snaking lineup.

"Stay," she said. Then left.

I waited in the lineup, eavesdropping on the conversations around me. Everyone in my line spoke Ukrainian.

"What is this place?" I asked the woman in front of me.

"The Red Cross," she answered. "Surely you know that."

"Yes, it's the Red Cross, but this isn't a hospital."

The woman smiled. "This office isn't to heal your body. It's to heal your soul."

"What do you mean?"

"Your loved ones," she said. "They can trace them for you."

Did that mean they would be able to find Mama and Tato and Lida? It seemed almost too good to be true.

I was nervous by the time it was finally my turn. I sat

down in front of a woman with lips painted the color of blood. She had a name tag, but it was written in English.

I held out my hand and said in Ukrainian. "I am Luka Barukovich. What is your name?"

"I'm Jean Smith from Wisconsin," she replied—in Ukrainian—as she tapped her name tag with an index finger. "But you can call me Genya."

"Thank you, Pani Genya," I said. "Can you find my parents, my friends? I can give you their names . . ."

"Hold on," said Genya. She ripped some forms off a pad and placed them in front of me. "We need to fill out one of these for each of your loved ones. We'll enter them onto our lists and circulate them through all of the DP camps. Then we hope for the best."

I picked up the pieces of paper and was about to leave, but Genya put one of her hands on mine. "It's okay," she said. "Stay here and I'll fill them out with you."

I began with my father.

"If he was taken to Siberia, we cannot help you," she said. "Our records only extend to the areas that were occupied by the Nazis."

Her words hit me like a hammer. Of course they wouldn't know. They had defeated the Nazis, but not the Soviets. How would I ever manage to find Tato? "My mother was taken as an *Ostarbeiter*," I said. "Can we start with her, then? Raisa Barukovich."

Genya's face brightened and she began to fill out one of the forms. "Yes. Do you have any information on where she was taken?"

"No, but I know when. She was taken from Kyiv during the last week in November 1942. The Nazis took us both at the same time, but we were put on two different trains."

"That helps a bit," said Genya. "We'll put it in our system."

"I am also looking for Lida Ferezuk."

"Is she also family?"

"No. A close friend. She was in the same labor camp as me."

"But you would have been liberated at the same time."

"No," I replied, considering how I would answer her. My escape from the camp and my time fighting in the Underground was something I didn't want to talk about yet. On the other hand, I needed to give Genya as much information as possible. "If you show me a map, I can point out where the camp was."

Genya got up and looked around, then came back with a big map of the Reich. Thank goodness Margarete and Helmut had shown me their actual location. "There," I said, my finger on an area close to the Oder River. "The work camp was somewhere in the countryside here. There was a bomb factory in a small town around there."

"That area is in Soviet control now," said Genya. "But by the time they arrived, that camp was emptied and the bomb factory destroyed."

"What does that mean?"

"Hard to say," replied Genya. "Leave it with me."

Time crawled in the days that followed, days that were some of the hardest I had ever lived through. I had become accustomed to action, to solving problems on my own. Now I was stuck waiting for others to do things for me. They gave me no responsibilities, and nothing to do. I felt so powerless.

All June, I occupied my time finding other Ukrainian-speaking refugees. "Have you heard of Lida Ferezuk or Raisa Barukovich?" I would ask. They'd shake their heads, then list off their own loved ones.

Other than that, I stood in lineups: for food, water, soap, showers. It got to the point that if I saw people lining up, I'd stand in line first and then ask what they were waiting for.

It was difficult to find a place to sleep. Every nook and

cranny of intact buildings and clear patch of ground had been claimed by someone. People would roll out their blankets and sleep just about anywhere. One night I slept in the back of a potato truck. Another time I slept sitting up, leaning against a wall.

Our camp was just down the road from another and another and another. I marveled that the Americans were able and willing and compassionate enough to help so many people. But how long could it go on? And without my parents or Martina or Lida, my life felt not worth living. Like so many others, I visited the other camps and asked everyone I met the same questions: *Have you heard of Lida Ferezuk or Raisa Barukovich? Do you know where they are?*

People began tacking up slips of paper at the entrances to the camps. On each one was a notice about loved ones, then a message about where the letter writer could be found. These slips of paper multiplied, fluttering in the wind like the furry pelt of a strange animal. I added my own, and each morning I checked the papers at the gates of every camp in my area.

Then one day, as I stood in a soup lineup, Genya came up to me, her eyes alight. "Why haven't you come back to see me, Luka?"

"I've been looking for my mother and Lida on my own."

"Well, come with me now. I have some information."

I followed her through a back door of the Red Cross building into what looked like a lunchroom for the staff. "Wait here," she said. "I'll be right back."

A man wearing a Red Cross badge on his white shirt eyed me suspiciously as he chewed on a cheese sandwich, but he didn't tell me to leave.

Genya came back, holding a manila envelope. As she sat across from me, she tore it open. "Twelve *Ostarbeiters* who were originally from Camp 14"—she looked up at me—"that camp your friend was at has been labeled Camp 14 by the Americans. Anyway, these *Ostarbeiters* were relocated to Bavaria and were liberated by the Americans in April. According to our information, one of them was named Lida Ferezuk."

I was so surprised by what she said that it took me a moment to digest it. "Lida's *alive*? And you know where she *is*?"

"She was very ill and was being treated in an American hospital in Austria until a few days ago. We can take you to the DP camp that she was released to—it's not that far from here. But remember, everyone goes from camp to camp, so I can't guarantee that she'll still be there."

CHAPTER TWENTY-FOUR
SUN-WASHED BARN

Genya got permission to drive me herself in a Red Cross van. "I'm dropping off supplies as well," she said. "So it just makes sense to take you with me."

The road was crowded with refugees, some coming to our camp and others leaving. Genya blasted her horn and nudged forward. A few people moved, but others ignored her. Some carried ragged suitcases, others pushed wheelbarrows. One woman balanced a wicker basket filled with jam jars on her head. I figured I could walk faster than Genya drove, but didn't want to hurt her feelings.

She drummed the steering wheel impatiently with her fingertips. "You'd probably get lost if you walked."

That made me smile. If only I could tell her all the places I had been.

I scanned the crowds as we inched forward. It was a good view from the high front seat of the van, so every time I saw a small girl with dark-blond hair, I'd watch until I could see her face. My biggest fear was that Lida would leave her DP camp before I got there and I'd lose track of her forever. Genya and I traveled for what seemed like hours.

"We're here," she said finally, drawing the van beside a crumbling stone entrance that was covered with the usual hundreds of fluttering papers—pinned to cracks, taped in a line, tied with string.

"You'd like to check the papers, I imagine," Genya said. "Good luck, and I hope you find your Lida."

"Thank you," I said, giving her a firm handshake. I opened the door and stepped out of the van. Genya waved as she drove inside the complex to drop off her supplies. I didn't stop to read the fluttering papers. I could do that anytime. Right now I had to find Lida. But how could I do that, among these thousands?

I walked down the dusty main roadway and looked carefully at each person I passed. What if Lida was taller now, or looked different after all this time? Would I even be able to recognize her?

As I passed one cluster of people after another, I realized that this camp seemed more permanent than the one I had come from. Maybe it was because the network of stone buildings still contained discernible rooms. So what if they had no coverings? Fractured families had settled into the corners of the large roofless rooms, some pitching makeshift tents for privacy, others living in the open, seemingly content with their invisible walls. A woman in a red bandanna crouched over a small charcoal fire that she'd lit in what had likely been a hallway, heating a lumpy, grayish liquid in a frying pan. A few buildings away, a grizzled old man sat on what was left of a stone wall and rocked a toddler as he sang a lullaby.

When I got to the end of the main street, I walked up the next street, then turned and walked down the next. Every now and then, amidst the hum of many languages, I'd hear people speaking Ukrainian. I'd stop and listen first, then ask if they knew Lida Ferezuk. No one did.

I did not stop looking until it got so dark I could no longer see. Had Genya been mistaken? Or perhaps Lida had been here but had left for a different camp. The thought of being so close to her, yet losing her again, overwhelmed me with sadness. I found a grassy spot against a tumbledown wall and fell into an uneasy sleep.

Early the next morning I felt a hand grip my shoulder. "Are you all right?"

I opened my eyes. A saggy-jowled woman with wild gray hair thrust half a slice of bread into my hands. "There's a lineup over there if you want more," she said, pointing.

I looked down at the bread, then back at the woman. It touched me that she would be so generous to a stranger. "Thank you."

"It's a new day," said the old woman. "Don't waste it." With that, she walked away.

I took a bite of the bread and chewed it slowly. She was right. Time to get up and look for Lida.

I walked up and down the same streets as I had the day before, stopping every time I heard someone speak Ukrainian. I would ask if they knew Lida Ferezuk. Just like yesterday, no one did.

But then a woman said, "You should try our church. We are all drawn to it sooner or later."

"There's a church?"

"This whole place used to be a convent," she said. "The chapel and church were destroyed, but we rebuilt ourselves a most beautiful Ukrainian church." She pointed to a barn at the edge of the camp, under a bank of trees. "It's there."

When I got closer to the barn, I began to have doubts. The building was so lopsided that it looked like it might collapse any minute, but there was a well-trod pathway leading right to it, and the door was open.

I stepped inside. Sunlight poured in from the holes in the roof, lighting up a rough wooden altar propped up on tin-can legs. In the center of the altar was an ancient icon of the Virgin Mary. I gasped at the sight of it. So much had been stolen from us that could never be returned, but at least this icon had been reclaimed.

On her knees before the altar was a small, thin girl with soft tufts of dark-blond hair. I would have known her anywhere.

I dared not breathe.

Lida whispered a prayer to the Virgin and I heard a list of names. One of them was my own.

I would have stepped forward and hugged her right then, but she was praying, and I didn't want to disturb her. Instead, I stood and watched in silence. On her feet were sturdy leather boots and that made me think of Martina's handmade boots—the ones that replaced her *postoly*.

I said a silent prayer myself—for Martina. She and Lida would have loved each other.

As Lida made the sign of the cross and began to stand up, I had a moment of doubt. Would she be happy to see me, or would she be angry that I had left her in the camp when I'd escaped?

She stumbled and nearly fell.

I dashed over and caught her elbow. "Let me help you."

Lida looked up, squinting in the sunlight. "Luka . . . ? *Luka!*"

"They told me I might find you here," I whispered. I

wanted to give her a kiss on the cheek, but I thought that might frighten her. Instead, I knelt in front of her and placed her arms around my neck and together we stood up.

"Dear Lida. I am so glad I found you."

Her arms were still wrapped around my neck and that was fine with me. She rested her head against my shoulder and it was the happiest moment of my life. But then I thought I heard a sob, and that got me worried. Maybe she wasn't really happy to see me. She took a deep breath, then said, "I dreamed of you the night you escaped."

So she wasn't angry, just sad. I had been thinking of her as well. Maybe we'd been thinking of each other at the exact same time? "I hated leaving you behind."

She took her arms from my neck so she could look me in the eye. "If you hadn't left when you did, I doubt you'd be alive now."

"And how did you stay alive?" I asked.

Her eyes clouded over. "It wasn't exactly easy," she said. Then she looked up at my face. "Sometimes you have to fight back."

I would have to ask her how she'd fought back, but not right now. And I would tell her about the Undergound— but not right now. Instead, we talked of the people we both knew from the camp: Julie's bravery and Zenia's escape.

"Have you found your sister?" I asked.

She shook her head. "Not yet." Then she said, "What about you? Have you found your parents?"

"No," I told her. "But the American Red Cross thinks they may be able to find Mama. After all, they found you."

Lida smiled at that. "I'm glad they did."

"It's my father I'm most worried about, though," I said. "With him being in Siberia, the Red Cross can't contact him."

Lida brushed a stray lock of hair from my cheek. "That may change."

As we walked out of the church together, I longed to hold Lida's hand, but I didn't know if she'd want me to. We talked about a thousand other things—I don't even know all that we said—just that I loved being with her. If I could keep her beside me for the rest of my life, I knew I'd be happy.

Over the next days and weeks, I spent every day with Lida. Together we helped families patch together temporary homes, assisted with first aid, and organized ball games with younger children. It was good to see these young boys and girls laughing out loud and running. After all the horrors they'd lived through, this was a gift for us as well as them. Lida's feet were weak and sometimes she stumbled, yet she never complained. But when her socks slipped down to her ankles, I saw her scars.

At night, we parted ways. I found a group of boys my age who also hadn't found their families. We took over a small room in one of the buildings toward the back of the complex. It had been overlooked by others because it had been entirely filled with rubble, but before my first night there was over, we organized one team to clear it out and another couple of boys to find us bedding and supplies.

Each morning, the first thing I'd do was to go find Lida. Together we would stand in line at the Red Cross. She was still looking for her younger sister, Larissa, and I was still waiting for news of my mother. Deep down, I hoped that by some miracle my father would be found as well. I had recently heard rumors of people who had been in Siberia, yet later turned up in refugee camps.

Larissa had only been five years old when she was taken. What were the chances that she had survived? That was a question I would never ask Lida. She lived in the hope of finding Larissa, just as I lived in the hope of finding my parents.

The adult Ukrainians set up schools and insisted that all Ukrainian children attend. I was offended to be treated this way. In years my age was only thirteen, but I had made bombs, assisted in surgery, and defended my country. Now

I was forced to sit on a bench with *children* and learn English grammar.

"But we need English," said Lida. "If we can get to England or Canada or America, that's what they speak there."

"Don't you want to go back home?" I asked her.

"I would love to," she said. "If I can find Larissa first, and if there is a home to go back to."

CHAPTER TWENTY-FIVE
HOME AGAIN

Weeks went by, and as July warmth turned to August swelter, we settled into a comfortable routine, but then one morning, two friendly looking Red Army soldiers waited patiently just inside my classroom door. One of them fidgeted with a piece of paper as we all streamed in and took our seats. Pan Semoniuk approached the door—a few minutes late as usual—and looked up in surprise when he noticed the Red Army men.

"Good morning, Comrades, can I help you?" Pan Semoniuk asked.

One of the soldiers stepped forward. His face broke out into an earnest smile. "Maybe," he said. "We would like to ask your students some questions."

Pan Semoniuk looked hesitant for a moment. "If you wish," he said finally.

The soldier walked into the middle of our class-room and faced us. He opened up his folded sheet. "I have information on family members for all of the following people. If you know who they are, please help me find them."

"Taras Melankovich?"

No one reacted.

"Mykola Boyko?"

No response.

"Ivan Tataryn?"

No response.

"Kost Chornij?"

A girl in the back of the class put up her hand. "He's not here," she said. "He's older than we are. But I know he's in this camp."

"Do you know where I can find him?"

"He helps out in the soup kitchen," she said. "Try there."

The soldier took a pencil out of his breast pocket and made a note. He looked up again and said, "Luka Barukovich?"

All eyes turned to me. I stood. The soldier grinned.

"I am glad to meet you, Luka. We have found a Volodymyr Barukovich, a pharmacist from Kyiv. Is that your father?"

"Yes!" I could hardly believe my ears. "Where is he?"

"Back in Kyiv," said the soldier. "He's been assigned the job of head pharmacist at State Pharmacy Number Four, and he'd like you to go back home to him."

"But don't the authorities consider me a traitor? I was captured by the Nazis."

"Haven't you heard?" asked the soldier, smiling. "There's been an amnesty. Stalin forgives you."

"What about my mother?"

The soldier looked at his paper. "Raisa Barukovich, correct?"

I nodded.

"We are looking for her. If she's still alive, we'll repatriate her when we find her. Your best course of action is to go home to Kyiv now. Pack up and be at the gate tomorrow morning."

I was so excited that I ran out to find Lida, but she was still in class, so I went back to my sleeping area and threw what little I had into my bag. Could it really be true? My father was alive! And they were searching for Mama. But what about Lida? I couldn't leave her behind, not now when I'd finally found her again.

The trick would be to convince her to come with me. That made the most sense, seeing as both her parents had died. The American Red Cross and the Soviet Red Cross could keep on looking for Larissa. We could give them our address in Kyiv. Once Larissa was found, she could come live with us. It would be perfect.

When Lida came out at lunch and we sat down together with our bowls of soup, I told her of my news. She was not at all happy for me. In fact, she seemed frightened.

"I don't believe this soldier," she said. "My teacher has heard some frightening stories of people who were hurt when they tried to go back. Do you really think that Stalin forgives that easily, after all he has done?"

"If it had been an NKVD agent who was trying to get me back, I'd be worried," I said. "But it's not. It's a Red Army soldier."

She didn't seem convinced, and her reluctance made me fume. I knew the difference between regular Red Army soldiers and NKVD agents. I had witnessed the difference in Kyiv and in the Underground. Red Army soldiers were conscripted. They were just regular people. The NKVD was the Soviet version of the Gestapo— trained killers.

"Perhaps you've been living with the Nazis for too long," I muttered. But as soon as the words were out, I wished I could have erased them.

Lida said nothing for a minute. I looked over at her

and saw that her knuckles were clenched white. "That is an *awful* thing to say to me."

"I'm sorry. I didn't mean it," I said. "But in the Undergound, we were fighting for everyone to be treated equally. That goes for Soviet soldiers too. Besides, don't they need workers for rebuilding after the war? It doesn't make sense for them to hold grudges."

"What about me?" Lida asked. Tears filled her eyes. "You've been gone for two years. I can't lose you again."

I set my bowl down and reached for her hand. "Please come with me. The Red Cross will keep on looking for Larissa and my mother, even after we've left here. And when they find Larissa, she can join us."

Lida was silent for a moment. Then she took a deep breath. "I don't trust that soldier. I think he's lying to you."

That was not how I saw it at all. Could she not understand how important it was for me to go to my father *now*? He was waiting for me. He had *asked* me to come. If I didn't go now, I might not get another chance to find him.

I could not believe how stubborn Lida was being about this. But I didn't want to keep on arguing. "I'm leaving tomorrow morning. I *have* to, Lida. Please understand," I told her.

Why couldn't Lida be excited for me? I had found my *father*! Couldn't she see why this was so important for me?

Finally, I said, "Come to say good-bye, or come with me. It's your choice."

She said nothing.

I grabbed my bowl of soup and stood up. I didn't know what to say. "See you later," I finally managed.

I spent the rest of the day wandering around the camp. I missed my old life. Soon I would be home, helping to make Kyiv whole again. If only Lida would come with me.

I got up before dawn and walked down to the gate. I watched the sun rise. Would Lida come with me? That was my dearest wish. I never wanted to be apart from her again. She was as much my family now as Mama and Tato.

But maybe she wouldn't even come and say good-bye.

Footsteps behind me, and then a voice. "You're going home too, Luka?" said Kost Chornij, the man from the soup kitchen. He set his satchel beside mine.

"I am."

"You don't look very happy about it."

"My friend Lida—I want her to come back with me, but she wants to stay here."

"Why don't you go find her? It's not even six o'clock yet. I'll watch your bag."

Lida had just stepped out of her door as I got there. Her eyes were red and her face looked tired. She was not carrying a bag.

"You've decided not to come with me?"

"I will see you off," she said. "But I'm staying here. I wish you would stay as well."

I stood there for a long moment, just staring at her. Why couldn't she realize how important it was for me to go back to my father right now? Did she not love me at all? I almost asked her that out loud, but I didn't want my memory of her to be spoiled with an argument. We walked in silence down to the entrance of the camp.

Kost Chornij wasn't the only one waiting anymore. There were two others.

"Taras Melankovich," said one man, holding out his hand. "And my cousin, Ivan Tataryn."

Lida seemed surprised that others were also going back. Would she change her mind at the last minute and come with me? I dared to ask once more if she would, but just then her teacher, Pani Zemluk, arrived. She touched Lida's shoulder.

"Lida, don't."

Lida took a deep breath, then turned to me. "Luka, I will not go with you. I want us to stay together forever. I want you to stay with me *now*—"

"I'm *not* staying here, I cannot," I told her.

"And I cannot go with you," she replied.

So that was it. Her choice was made.

I hugged her one last time. "Stay safe, sister of my heart. Maybe one day, you and your sister will join us."

"I would like that," she said, her voice choked with tears.

Just then a canvas-covered Red Army truck careened to a stop and that same soldier stepped out. He grabbed a clipboard and ticked off the names, then his eyes focused on Lida. "And who are you? Are you coming home with us today?"

Lida's mouth opened, but no sound came out. For a moment I thought maybe she had changed her mind. She blinked, then said, "I need to find my sister first."

"The Soviet Red Cross can help with that. What is your sister's name and where were you two born?"

Lida was about to tell him, but Pani Zemluk squeezed her shoulder and said, "Children should be seen and not heard."

Lida looked at me, her eyes pleading. "*Please*, Luka, stay here with me."

Why couldn't she understand? If our positions were reversed, would she turn her back on her own father? Why wouldn't she just come with me? It would be perfect if she'd do that. All I could say was "I must go back. My father is waiting for me."

I climbed into the back of the truck. Kost stepped in behind me, and then the other two. As the truck sped away, I watched through a gap in the canvas as Lida got smaller and smaller.

CHAPTER TWENTY-SIX
FREIGHT

I had expected the road to be clogged with refugees, but in the direction we were going, it was nearly empty. The driver careened around potholes and puddles with deft last-minute turns while he hummed the Soviet national anthem under his breath. After a few miles, he pulled over to the side of the road and we all got out for a bit of fresh air.

"You can call me Yurij," said the soldier. "I've got some good *kolbassa* here."

He dug into a cloth sack and brought out a long coil of the sausage. "And strong cheese." He pulled a knife from his back pocket and sliced *kolbassa* and cheese for each of us.

I took a small bite of the *kolbassa* and broke off a bit of cheese. The five of us joked and laughed. I was feeling good about my decision to go back.

"Luka," said Yurij, his smile suddenly gone. He handed

me a second slice of *kolbassa*. "You escaped the *Ostarbeiter* camp a while ago, didn't you?"

I tried to swallow the cheese and meat, but it got stuck in my throat.

"No reason to be nervous," he said. "What did you do after that?"

I looked at the soldier again. Yurij's uniform was Red Army, but his curiosity seemed more like NKVD. Petro had told me that I'd know when the time was right to talk about the UPA, and this was certainly *not* the time. "I hid in the woods."

"Okay," he growled. "If that's how you want to play this game, it's fine with me. Time to go back to the truck."

Once we began moving again, Kost leaned in to me and whispered. "Were you in the Ukrainian Insurgent Army?"

His question surprised me. I didn't answer right away.

"I was in it too," he said. "In the forests of Polissia." He scooted over to the other side of the truck and whispered, "Taras, Ivan, were you in the Underground?"

Ivan shook his head. "I was a slave laborer in a quarry."

"I was an *Ostarbeiter* right up until my camp was liberated by the Americans," said Taras.

We didn't talk anymore. I closed my eyes and tried to get a little bit of sleep. Finally the truck stopped and Yurij pulled the canvas back so we could get out. He had parked in front of an old brick-and-stone train station. The building itself had been bombed, but the rubble was cleared away now and the station was clearly still functioning. There were American troops stationed on our side of the depot, and Soviet troops on the other side of the tracks.

"Come in to the depot," said Yurij. "The Soviet Zone begins just beyond the doorstep."

I was the last to walk through. As soon as the door closed behind us, Yurij punched me hard in the gut three times. I doubled over and nearly fell. "Don't be so slow the next time," he said. Then he took a pistol from his belt and pointed to the far corner with it. "Stand there."

Kost grabbed my arm and helped me, so all four of us got to the corner at the same time, stunned by the abrupt change. Moments later I was still gasping for breath.

The door opened again and a dozen people were herded in—mostly men, but in this group there were two women and three children as well. "Stand with those men," said a different soldier who had ushered them in.

We all stood, chilled by the change in attitude, wondering what was going to happen next. And then the door opened again and a third group of people stepped in—six—all my age. Two were girls. One of the boys was Andrij, the villager whom Viktor and I had saved from the Nazi death camp. His group was shuttled over to stand with us as well,

224

and he noticed me right away. When the soldiers were talking among themselves, I edged over to him.

"Andrij," I whispered. "I'm surprised you're going back. Do you have family there?"

"This wasn't my decision. They picked me up and threw me into the truck," he whispered. "I have to get out of here."

More Soviet soldiers streamed in, swaggering and joking with Yurij. One wearing a gray NKVD uniform and carrying a clipboard seemed to be in charge.

"If I read your name, step forward," he said. "Kost Chornij, Taras Melankovich, Yevhen Marunchak . . ."

The six stepped forward one by one. They were all forty years or older. Five men and one woman.

"You are all traitors to the Motherland," the NKVD policeman said in a low, controlled voice. "You will suffer for your transgressions."

Still staring at the men, the policeman raised one hand and snapped his fingers. Yurij and the other soldiers, on cue, fell upon the six: punching them in the face, tearing out hair, kicking them in the groin. The lone woman was dragged by her hair and kicked in the ribs. I watched in horror as a boot landed on Kost's face.

"Too messy," said the NKVD boss in a bored voice. "Finish this outside."

Soldiers collared the prisoners and dragged them out the door opposite the one we had come through—out to the Soviet side.

Six shots rang out.

I was in utter shock. The beating was one thing, but this . . . What had I gotten myself into? Andrij edged closer to me, but I was frozen to the spot, still gasping for breath.

The door on the Soviet side opened, and the soldiers came back in, without their prisoners. Each wore a smirk of satisfaction on his face.

One of the girls screamed.

"Go ahead—all of you—and scream if you want," said the NKVD boss, pacing in front of us. "You're in the Soviet Zone now. The Americans might hear you, but they can't come to your rescue."

The group of soldiers crossed the room and waded into our group. A punch to the head dropped me to the ground. Heavy boots kicked my ribs and someone tore my satchel out of my hands. Someone else pulled off my boots. "You won't need these where you're going," I heard through the shouts and screams.

All around me, women, children, and men cried out as they were kicked and hit. Suddenly everything went black.

I woke to a rhythmic chugging and the smell of many people cramped together. I tried to sit up, but my head swirled. "Where am I?"

"On a train to Siberia," said a woman's voice.

I opened my eyes. As they got used to the shadows, I saw stark wooden walls and the other captives who'd been beaten with me. A woman with a swollen eye sat in the corner, singing to a weeping child. Several men stood together in a cluster, talking in animated tones. Andrij sat close to me on the floor, holding his forearm at an awkward angle.

I propped myself up and said to Andrij, "Is your arm broken?"

"Maybe," he said in a strained voice.

I felt his arm above the wrist and found a fracture in the ulna. The bone had not broken through the skin, and the second bone, the radius, felt intact. This was very good. But the broken edges of the ulna were at an awkward angle and if they were not aligned, Andrij's arm could not mend properly. Without warning, I swiftly pulled on Andrij's arm and realigned the broken ends. He screamed.

"Does anyone have a stick?" I asked the others.

227

The men stopped talking. The woman stopped singing. The child kept on weeping.

"They took everything from us," said the woman. "Where would we get a stick?"

"I need something to splint Andrij's arm with."

One of the men reached into his shirt and pulled out a sheaf of handwritten letters. He flipped through them one last time and his eyes filled with tears. Then he took a deep breath and rolled them into a tight tube. As he passed the papers to me, he said, "I'm Mykola. Here's your splint."

I could only imagine who the letters were from. His wife? His children? "Thank you," I said. "I'll also need a strip of cloth."

The woman in the corner tore a narrow strip from her skirt and handed it to Mykola. I positioned the tube along Andrij's forearm as a splint, then secured it with the strip of cloth. Andrij's face was etched with pain, but he nodded his thanks.

A man reached down and pulled me to a standing position. "That was kind of you to help that boy and I give you my sincere thanks. But we've got urgent business right now and we'd like you to have a say in it."

The other men nodded.

"I am going to escape," said Mykola, pointing to a spot close to the floor on one of the walls. "There's an opening right there that's been nailed shut. We're going to pry it open."

I walked over to the spot and looked closely. Sure enough, the outline of what used to be an opening was clear, but now it was covered with wood and tightly nailed shut.

"When we were being taken in," Mykola said, "I noticed that on the outside, that spot is covered with barbed wire. Not such a problem for us to break through. Near that is a bumper beam and a coupler that attaches to the next boxcar. If we can reach it, we could jump when the train slows down a bit."

"But what about our families back home?" I said. "I'd be willing to go to Siberia for a little while if it meant that I could reunite with my family at some point."

Mykola's eyes suddenly looked like a light had been extinguished from them. "You don't remember what they told you about your father?"

"My fath—?"

"You must have still been partly unconscious. My family, your father . . . They're dead. It was just bait to get us back for punishment."

His words took a moment to sink in. And then I did remember, even if the memory of it was still hazy.

How could I have been so stupid? I had abandoned Lida and also the chance of finding my own mother. And for what? To chase the dream that my father was still alive? The reality of it all hit me in the gut. I could never go home.

I had nothing.

But at least I had nothing to lose.

The plan sounded dangerous, but so was Siberia. And I had to get back to Lida.

"You can't go without boots," said Andrij. "Take mine."

"I can't take your boots, Andrij. Aren't you coming with us?"

He held up his arm. "Do you really think I could make it with a broken arm? I would just hold the rest of you up. I'll have to take my chances with the Soviets."

He unlaced his boots with his one good hand and gave them to me. "Take them," he said. "You saved my life twice. This is the least I can do."

I had very mixed feelings about it, but in the end, I did take his boots. "Who else will be escaping?" I asked.

Mykola raised his hand. A few others.

It didn't take long to break through the wood and nails. Half a dozen prisoners slid Mykola feet first out the opening. I offered to help, but they told me to save my strength. I watched as he clung on, his arms and shoulders on our side and everything else outside. He slowly maneuvered himself outside. Soon, only his fingers showed, then nothing at all.

The train's chugging was too loud to let us know what Mykola's fate was on the other side. They slid me out next. When most of my body was outside and I could feel the wind whipping around me, I looked at everyone in the boxcar one last time. "Thank you," I said. "God be with you all." And then I pulled my head outside the boxcar.

It was daylight. Mykola stood on the bumper, his hands clutching the side of the boxcar. I maneuvered myself over to him, with one foot on the coupler and the other on the bumper. With one hand I grabbed on to a metal bar.

The ground below us fell away at a dizzying speed. How could we ever jump? But Mykola crouched down and concentrated. "Good luck," he said. Then jumped.

A smacking sound. A scream. I cleared my mind and concentrated on what I had to do.

I stepped over to where Mykola had stood and bent forward to see if I could get a view beyond the train car. Up ahead was a bridge underpass. Not a good time to jump. After we went through it, the train slowed as it climbed a hill.

I jumped.

My knees buckled and I fell as my feet hit the ground. I hugged my arms around my chest and rolled—careening down an embankment at a dizzying speed. I was barely able to stop myself just before crashing into a tree. I stood up, but nearly fell over again because I was so dizzy. My arms were a network of scratches and when I touched my cheek, my hand came away bloody, but I hadn't broken any bones.

I pushed away the twigs and stones, then began walking back, keeping hidden behind the brush, my eyes peeled for Mykola. He must have been injured, but I couldn't be sure how badly.

And then I saw him—splayed out like a broken doll on a jutting rock, his skull crushed to a pulp. He had been so close to freedom and now he was dead. The person whose letters he'd cherished would never know of his death.

I dragged his body off the rock and hid it amidst some bushes. I couldn't give him a proper burial, but I covered his body with some stones, then grabbed a handful of dirt and sprinkled it over him. I knelt down beside him and kissed his hand, then in a low, whispering voice, I sang the *Vichnaya Pamyat*—"Eternal Memory."

I would never forget Mykola.

I began the long walk back to the train depot with one thought: I had to get back to Lida. I was still woozy from my fall and from being beaten, but Andrij's boots saved my life. I still felt guilty, though. How could he get by in a Soviet prison camp without boots?

NKVD agents patrolled the tracks, so I had to stay hidden and time my movements to theirs. When I finally reached the train depot, I was nearly dead from fatigue.

As I hid nearby, I waited for a time to cross. It finally came when another group of prisoners was beaten, then loaded onto a train. After that train left, the soldiers got so drunk they passed out. I walked across the tracks and sneaked into the American sector.

I was dizzy with exhaustion but forced myself to stay awake and keep on moving until the depot was out of sight. What kept me going were thoughts of Lida. I accepted that my father was dead. I had no choice. My mother? I would keep on looking. But of all the people in the world, there was only one whom I could not live without: Lida.

I collapsed onto the road. An American military truck stopped and loaded me into the back. "We'll take you to the hospital," said a soldier.

"No," I said. "I need to get back to my camp."

CHAPTER TWENTY-SEVEN
BACK TO LIDA

The next hours were a blur. I didn't remember the trip. I must have lost consciousness, because when I did come to, I was in what looked like a hospital room. My ragged clothing was gone and in its place was a hospital gown. Clean gauze covered my arms and legs. At first I was devastated. They hadn't listened to me. They'd taken me to a hospital instead of back to Lida.

But then I felt a cool sponge on my forehead and I heard Lida's familiar voice. "You're safe, dear Luka."

I looked up. Lida's face hovered over me, her eyes swollen and red. I tried to sit up, but I was so woozy that I fell back down. "Lida, can you ever forgive me for leaving you?"

She brushed my cheek with her fingertips. "There is nothing to forgive, Luka."

"My father . . . he's dead. The whole thing was a trick.

You were right all along. I am so glad that you didn't try to come back with me."

Her eyes filled with tears. She took one of my hands in hers and kissed it. "I am so sorry about your father."

Neither of us said anything for quite some time. My body ached from the bruises and scrapes, and my heart was filled with sorrow for the loss of my father, but lying there with Lida's hands wrapped around my own was like a salve for the soul. Lida was not angry with me. She understood.

"Don't ever leave me, Lida," I said.

She didn't say anything for a full minute, and during that time I wondered what she was thinking. Then her lips trembled into a smile. "I am here. I will not leave you."

Those words brought me up short. Of course she was right. It had always been me chasing after my past when my future was right here in front of me—with Lida.

"I'll never leave you again, Lida. That is a promise." Her hands were still wrapped around mine, and it took all the strength I had to raise one of her hands to my lips. I kissed her fingertips.

"I love you, Lida. And I always will."

"I love you too," she said. "You are the other half of me."

She gently laid her head upon my bruised shoulder,

and the weight of it hurt, but I didn't care. I wrapped one arm around her back as best I could and kissed her on the top of her head. "You are my life, my home, my soul."

I barely had time to heal before I knew it was time to leave. The Soviets might find me again.

Pani Zemluk agreed. "They will be back for you, Luka," she said. "Of that I have no doubt."

Lida and I fled to the British zone. Hiding in plain sight with many others who were just like us, we walked for weeks and weeks. We scanned thousands of fluttering notes, looking for information about Lida's sister and my mother, but we never found anything. My deepest fear was that both of them were dead. But Lida and I had each other and I was grateful for that. We carved out happiness where we could in our vagabond existence. As I looked around at the hordes of refugees, lost and ragged, searching for loved ones, searching for home, I felt lucky. No matter what, I had Lida. And as long as we were together, life was worth living.

EPILOGUE

We each had skills, so we eked out an existence in the British DP camp. Lida developed a never-ending list of customers vying for her stitch work. There were many displaced persons, all needing a country to emigrate to, and all wanting to look presentable for their interviews. Lida helped them do that.

Mr. Schaefter, a German pharmacist, hired me as an apprentice. I didn't earn as much as Lida did with her sewing, but Hans kindly taught me all he knew. He was also interested in my family's traditional remedies, as well as the ones I had learned on my own while on the run and in the Underground.

Five years later, our lives had not changed. We were forever poised for a future that never seemed to happen. We could not find my mother or Larissa. And it seemed that no country wanted us.

Then the next year, Lida found Larissa. Or should I say that Larissa found her? A letter arrived from Canada. And an invitation from Larissa and her adoptive parents asking Lida to join them in Canada. The thought of Lida leaving tore me to the quick, but reuniting with her sister was her dream come true. "I am so happy for you," I told her.

She pulled back from me just a little bit and looked me in the eye. "I made you promise that you wouldn't leave me, Luka," she said. "Do you think I would leave *you*? Where I go, you go."

"And my mother?"

"We won't stop looking for your mother just because we're in Canada."

That night I tossed and turned in bed, thinking of what our future would hold. My future was with Lida and her family—in Canada. But before we left, there was one thing I had to do. We were old enough. It was time.

I visited a local jeweler and asked what she had in the way of wedding rings. She pulled out a velvet tray of gold bands. The ones I could afford were all previously owned—that brought back disturbing memories. But some of the new rings were silver. I picked out a delicate silver ring with a pattern that looked like a wreath of lilacs. It was perfect.

That evening, I walked to Lida's boardinghouse.

When she opened the door, I got down on one knee and held out the ring. "Will you marry me, Lida?"

She pulled me up until I was standing and wrapped her arms around me. "Yes, Luka," she said. "I will marry you!"

It was the happiest day of my life.

A year later, the sleek Canadian train we were riding on shuddered to a stop at the Brantford station. Lida looked up at me, her eyes shining. I grabbed our luggage from the storage bin above—just a thin suitcase between us.

I searched the waiting crowd on the platform, recognizing Larissa right away. She stood there, looking so much like Lida, holding a bouquet of fresh lilacs. She was a bit shorter and her hair was blonder, but the eyes, the nose, the smile—the same.

The two hugged and wept for joy. "I would never have found you without the help of Marusia and Ivan," said Larissa.

I hadn't noticed the couple standing to the side. "You must be Luka," the woman said. "Welcome to Canada." The man beside her introduced himself as Ivan and held out his hand. I shook it firmly.

We five stood awkwardly for a moment, everyone but Lida a stranger to me. As we drove away from the station, a jumble of emotions ran through me. I was glad that Lida had found her sister, and grateful that Marusia and Ivan had helped me get to Canada, but as happy as I was for Lida, I longed for a little bit of the same joy. Tato and Dido were dead. Martina and David too. Would I ever find my mother? Ever truly be at home? How would I fit into this world?

"We're here," said Ivan, pulling the car into the driveway of a small wooden house. Walking inside was like stepping back in time. There was a familiar scent of chicken soup simmering in the kitchen, and a faint breeze filled with lilac.

The five of us sat down to a simple meal of soup with dumplings and fresh rye bread. I was overwhelmed by how normal life was for Marusia and Ivan. I knew that they had lived through the war, and that Larissa especially had experienced terrible things, but somehow they had been able to put it behind them, to carry on with their lives. I looked up from my plate to find Marusia smiling at me.

"We have so much in common, Luka," she said. "And a whole future of dreams ahead of us. I have a feeling you'll be happy here."

Her words had the ring of truth. I turned and caught Lida's eye, then smiled. Yes, I would be happy.

AUTHOR'S NOTE

MY NOVEL *Making Bombs for Hitler* introduces the reader to two young sisters who were captured by the Nazis but suffered dramatically different fates.

Luka is also captured by the Nazis, but when he escapes, his story lets the reader step into the world of a brave group of people who fought not just the Nazis but the Soviets as well.

I first heard about the Ukrainian Insurgent Army (UPA) almost two decades ago. Could it really be true that there was an underground army that fought the two most bloodthirsty dictatorships of the twentieth century? People who couldn't take the tyranny anymore, so they went into the woods and the mountains, built hiding places and underground hospitals, and fought back for freedom, even though they'd likely die in the process?

I still hardly believed it—until 1999, when I met Peter J. Potichnyj, Professor Emeritus of Political Science at McMaster University. He had joined the UPA when he was fourteen. Not only has he written his own story, but he has been collecting primary documents about the UPA for decades and is the editor in chief of Litopys UPA, a set of documents and memoirs about the UPA, which comprises 115 volumes, mostly in Ukrainian.

Without Peter's guidance, I would not have been able to write this book.

The battles and incidents that Luka and Martina are involved in during the time of this story are based on actual events. Luka and Martina are fictional characters inspired by real people, and the villages are fictionalized but based on real ones.

The framework of Luka's story relies on some key historical events:

Babyn Yar is a ravine located in Kyiv, beside a Jewish cemetery. Over the course of two days, September 29 and 30, 1941, the Nazis killed 33,771 Jews at this site. This was one of the largest single massacres in World War II. By the end of the war, Babyn Yar would claim more than 100,000 other Nazi victims, including Roma, Ukrainians, and Soviet prisoners of war.

Bykivnia was a village in the woods on the northeastern fringe of Kyiv. Between 1936 and 1941, the Soviets used the area as a massive yet secret burial ground. More than 100,000 Ukrainians and others who had been tortured and killed by the NKVD are buried there.

Forced repatriation occurred after the war, when Stalin demanded that Soviet citizens who had, in Stalin's eyes, "allowed themselves" to be captured by the Nazis be returned to the Soviet Union. Those who did return were either killed outright or sent to brutal work camps in Siberia, because Stalin considered anyone who was captured by the Nazis to be a traitor. Those who managed to escape to the West hid their wartime experiences because they feared being sent back to the Soviet Union. Their stories began to emerge only after the 1991 dissolution of the Soviet Union.

NKVD was the Communist secret police, a brutal organization whose task was to inflict terror on perceived enemies of the Soviet Union.

Ostarbeiter (Eastern worker) was the name the Nazis gave to the millions of young people, many from what is now Eastern Ukraine, who were forced into labor. They were required to wear a badge stitched with the letters *OST.* Most lived behind barbed wire in guarded camps. The 3 to 5.5 million *Ostarbeiters* in Nazi Germany were treated harshly—often worked to death. Many were forced to work in German munitions factories because the Nazis realized that those were prime targets for bombing by the Allied nations and did not want to risk their own citizens.

Joseph Stalin was the dictator of the Soviet Union from about 1924 until his death in 1953. During the winter of 1933–1934, he withdrew food from Eastern Ukraine and sealed the borders so that the populace starved to death by the millions. This act of genocide is now known as the *Holodomor*—literally "death by hunger."

Koreans, Poles, Germans, Chechens, Tatars, and other ethnic groups were deported from their homelands to prison camps in Siberia, Central Asia, and other harsh, remote regions, where large numbers of them died. Stalin ordered so-called "socially harmful people" such as the homeless, the unemployed, and former aristocracy to be shot.

It is impossible to know how many people were killed as a result of Stalinism. Estimates range from 15 to 20 million or more.

For the first two years of World War II, Stalin fought on the same side as Hitler, against the Allies. After Hitler attacked the Soviet Union in June 1941, the Allies accepted Stalin on their side.

The **Ukrainian Insurgent Army** (Ukrainska povstanska armiia, or UPA) was a well-organized military network of guerrilla fighters—men and women whose goal was independence for Ukraine. The UPA fought both the

Nazis and the Soviets and operated throughout Ukraine, but were mostly concentrated in Volyn, the Carpathian Mountains, and forests of Western Ukraine. The UPA was formed in response to the brutality of both regimes and drew its members from many nationalities and all parts of the populace, although most of its members were Ukrainian. At its height, the army numbered between 45,000 and 60,000 fighters.

READ MORE ABOUT LIDA IN

MAKING BOMBS FOR HITLER

A novel by **MARSHA FORCHUK SKRYPUCH**

CHAPTER ONE
LOSING LARISSA—1943

The room smelled of soap and the light was so white that it made my eyes ache. I held Larissa's hand in a tight grip. I was her older sister, after all, and she was my responsibility. It would be easy to lose her in this sea of children, and we had both lost far too much already.

Larissa looked up at me and I saw her lips move, but I couldn't hear her words above the wails and screams. I bent down so that my ear was level with her lips.

"Don't leave me," she said.

I wrapped my arms around her and gently rocked her back and forth. I whispered our favorite lullaby into her ear.

A loud crack startled us both. The room was suddenly silent. A woman in white stepped in among us. She clapped her hands sharply once more.

"Children," she said in brisk German. "You will each have a medical examination."

Weeping boys and girls were shoved into a long snaking line that took up most of the room. I watched as one by one, kids were taken behind a broad white curtain.

When it was Larissa's turn, her eyes went round with fright. I did not want to let go of her, but the nurse pulled our hands apart.

"Lida, stay with me."

I stood at the edge of the curtain and watched as the woman made Larissa take off her nightgown. My sister's face was red with shame. When the woman held a metal instrument to her face, Larissa screamed. I rushed up and tried to knock that thing out of the nurse's hand, but the nurse called for help and someone held me back. When they finished with Larissa, they told her to stand at the other end of the room.

When it was my turn, I barely noticed what they were doing. I kept my eyes fixed on Larissa. She was standing with three other girls. Dozens more had been ordered to stand in a different spot.

When the nurse was finished with me, I slipped my nightgown back on. I was ordered to stand with the larger group—not with Larissa's.

"I need to be in that group," I told the nurse, pointing to where Larissa stood, her arms outstretched, a look of panic on her face.

ABOUT THE AUTHOR

MARSHA FORCHUK SKRYPUCH is a Ukrainian Canadian author acclaimed for her nonfiction and historical fiction, including *Making Bombs for Hitler*, a companion to this novel. She was awarded the Order of Princess Olha by the president of Ukraine for her writing. Marsha lives in Brantford, Ontario, and you can visit her online at www.calla.com.